JOURNEY INTO DARKNESS

a story in four parts

part 1

On the Eve of Conflict

part 2

Up From Corinth

part 3

Across the Valley to Darkness

part 4

Toward the End of the Search

ACROSS THE VALLEY TO DARKNESS

book three of
JOURNEY INTO DARKNESS

written by
J. Arthur Moore

Author's Note:

Journey Into Darkness was begun some years ago. It is finally being written at the request of Charley French, one of several campers who heard the story while on camping trips with the author. Learning the original story had not been worked on for some time, he offered to represent the main character if the author would continue to work on the story. So for him and others who have enjoyed the telling of *Journey Into Darkness* this book is written.

Another camper, Michael Flanagan, suggested the format of the story. On behalf of the many young readers who do not like thick books, he felt several smaller books would be more appropriate. Therefore the story of *Journey Into Darkness* is told in a series of four books.

All photography is by the author. Duane Kinkade is represented by Charlie French; Tod Gardner is represented by Matthew Oswald; and Johnny Applebee is represented by David Rowland. All youngsters are participants in camping programs directed by the author.

Library of Congress Control Number: 2013905484
ISBN: Hardcover   978-1-4836-1586-8
                 Softcover   978-1-4836-1585-1
                 Ebook   978-1-4836-1587-5

This is a work of historic fiction. An intricate blend of fact and fiction, the thread of experience of the fictitious boy soldier runs through the fabric of a very real war and its historic violence exactly as it happened.

This book was printed in the United States of America.

Rev. date: 03/27/2013

To order additional copies of this book, contact:
Xlibris Corporation
1-888-795-4274
www.Xlibris.com
Orders@Xlibris.com
133370

Dedication

Across the Valley to Darkness is dedicated in His love to Charley French, Matthew Oswald, and David Rowland, each of whom has helped by becoming forever a part of the story through the photographic material, and to all who have enjoyed its telling and shared in the adventure of its creation.

Duane Kinkade

Tod Gardner

Johnny Applebee

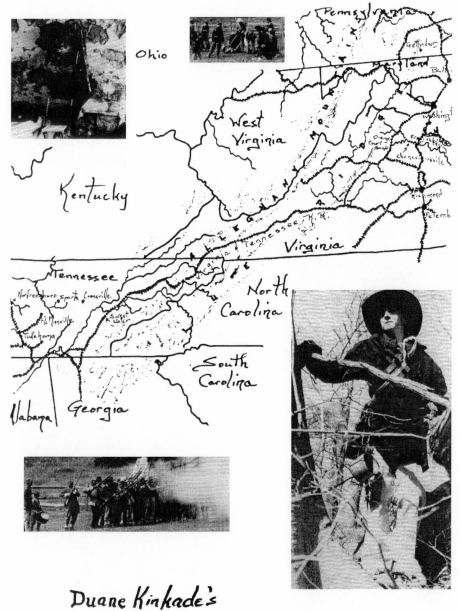

Duane Kinkade's
journeys
1863

A light snow swirled gently in the afternoon air, carpeting the countryside in new powder. The lone figure of the boy plodded along the empty dirt lane that was the main road, hardly visible in whirling whiteness. The chill air bit through his layers of clothing, and the confusing visibility made it impossible for him to keep his bearings. Duane paused to rewrap the scarf across his face as a new wind whipped about the back of his neck. Somewhere the road forked right toward Tullahoma. But it couldn't be seen. The boy listened to the snowy silence for some sound of life, then moved on.

Two years ago Duane was just another farm boy back in Arkansas. Then the war had come and his pa had left to fight for the Confederacy. During the months of summer his mother had been killed by raiders and he had been left for dead. Christmas came. It was lonely without his parents. Only his dog was left of the family he loved. Then, during the lonely months of winter, the letter had come. His pa was in Tennessee, but had no idea as to the events in his family's life.

Suddenly, the boy had to find his pa. Thus it was he left to become part of the fabric of war. As drummer boy in an Arkansas regiment, he fell at Shiloh to be found by a Union surgeon and his teenaged ward. The balance of the year was spent with the Union Army until the bloody battle at Murfreesboro. Alone on the battlefield, Duane had decided the time had come to go in search of the Confederate Army of which he had learned his pa's regiment was a part.

Duane had been alone on the road since morning when he'd left the outskirts of Murfreesboro behind to seek the Confederate Army encampment at Tullahoma. The Tennessee countryside was empty of activity this first full week of January, since most had settled in to ride out the first snows of the new year. The boy's thoughts drifted back to last week and the terrible battle that had snuffed out so many lives. He thought of the friends he'd left behind in the hope that in just a few days he would find the Confederate Army and be reunited with his father. Now he wasn't so sure he'd made the right decision. Every time he felt he was close, something happened to change the course of his plans.

A distant clatter intruded on his thoughts and the boy paused to listen. Quickly it approached from the road behind. Suddenly, ghostlike, it burst into view, materializing from the snowy atmosphere. A frenzied young driver pushed his panicked horse as though racing his flatbed wagon against the devil himself. Duane jumped out of the way, his sudden movement startling the wagoneer who hauled his beast up short.

"Git on quick!" the youngster shouted. "There's Yanks comin up fast!"

The foot-weary boy clambered aboard without pause as the driver slapped his horse into a run. Duane grabbed the seat mount as the vehicle lurched forward, nearly throwing him off the back.

"How many?" Duane asked, drawing himself up on the back of the seat board.

"Dunno really, but two fer sher." The younger boy, perhaps ten years old, was dressed warmly in an overcoat with his hat brim pulled down over his ears and held firmly in place with his scarf. Stretching forward with the reins held tightly between his fingers, the boy urged his horse to ever greater speed.

Duane managed to hug tightly the back of the seat as the force of the racing vehicle pulled at his grip. Snow stung his face. His gear slapped against his back or slipped awkwardly from his shoulder to his elbow.

"Why fer'd ya pick me up?" Duane shouted into the wind.

"Ya'r one a us, ain't ya?" the boy responded without turning his attention from his horse. "These Yanks ain't 'zactly friendly." Shifting his feet to brace himself, he continued, "Hang tight. We turn here."

With that, the young driver yanked the reins and the horse veered hard to the left, throwing the spinning wheels into a sideways slide. The beast was strong. He pulled the wagon out of its skid without breaking stride and disappeared into a snowy

16

lane, nearly hidden by white-covered vegetation. Soft powder billowed about the moving mass, kicked up by the swirling motion, dusting the boys and their vehicle in white. A quarter mile along the lane, the horse was pulled from his wild run and allowed to trot briskly the remaining few hundred feet into a small farm yard.

"My name's Thomas," the boy introduced.

"Call me Dee," Duane acknowledged.

"Okay, Dee." He halted the rig. "Help me unhitch an run the wagon inta the shed. Then dust it with dirt 'n straw while I hide 'Ol Jake in the lean-to out back."

The two unhitched the harness for the wagon and rolled the rig backwards into the shed. Duane watched Thomas lead the horse out of sight behind the small frame house, then turned to do as he'd been asked. Several minutes passed. Duane finished, found a small bucket, and made a seat to await the other boy's return.

He studied the house, silent in the snow, its chimney smoke blending into the falling flakes. As he watched, Thomas appeared at the corner of the house, peering cautiously down the lane. The young boy motioned for Duane to look, then ducked out of sight. Duane glanced as directed and saw two mounted figures advancing slowly in the snowfall. Quickly, he slipped along the back wall of the shed to conceal himself in the dark shadows behind the strawpile, as a gust of wind whipped through the shed to dust over the footprints just left by the boys. There he hoped to watch in safety.

Cautiously the two entered the stillness of the farmyard. One grizzled cavalryman guided his mount along the front of the shed. He paused to study the wagon and glance about the shadows, then turned to join his stocky companion near the door to the farm house. As the bearded rider dismounted and approached the farm house, his fat companion reached for his rifle which hung on its swivel harness and brought it to bear on the house door.

The door opened to the knock and a tall homely woman stood there, surrounded by three small children. Duane couldn't hear the conversation, but he did hear the children's screams when the soldier slapped their mother and threw her to the ground. Angry voices made demands, but the woman remained seated in the snow.

The boy checked his musket, placed a cap on the nipple and cocked the hammer. His pistol was ready. Laying the weapon across the straw, he took aim on the mounted rider and waited.

Raised voices carried on the snowy breeze.

"We know that wagon just come in, M'am, and we aim to take the horse! There's no use to be stubborn, cause we can be stubborn, too!"

"Ya's git from here an leave be! We ain't left with no livestock cause ya'all's done made off with ever'thin we got."

The other rasped, "Woman, we either get that horse or we might take to burnin you out."

The woman moved to get up, but was pushed back to the snow by a muddy boot.

"Leave my ma be!" a small girl shrieked as she pommeled the soldier on his leg with her small fists.

"Ha!" he laughed as he pushed the child into the snow with the woman.

Suddenly a gunshot flashed through a window and Duane knew he had to act. He squeezed the trigger as the mounted soldier swung in the saddle to fire into the house. No one was hit, but the second soldier grabbed his rifle as the woman shooed her little ones into the house and quickly crawled after them. A shot ripped the door frame as they disappeared within and the soldiers fired in confusion. Duane fired wildly with his revolver, hoping to scare the two off. It worked. The thin one mounted hastily and the two rode anxiously down the lane.

After a moment of silence, Duane holstered his revolver, picked up his musket, and stepped from behind the straw pile. The door to the house opened and Thomas stepped out.

"Hey, Dee! Ya git yerself in here real fast-like!"

Duane dashed through the snowfall and disappeared into the house.

The first thing the boy noticed within the dwelling was the warmth. It wrapped him in a comfort he hadn't felt since leaving the Widow Smith's. His vision grew accustomed to the dimness and he realized all eyes were on him. The little ones huddled in uncertainty behind their mother's skirt while their older brother stood with eyes dancing in hero-worship. Anger flashed in the woman's cutting glare as she sized up this stranger from head to foot.

"Ya had no cause fer sech unchristian-like behavin, Boy." Her hands caressed the small heads at her side.

"But, Ma!" Thomas defended. "Dee, here saved us from them Yanks."

Duane stood silently uncertain as the woman continued. "It ain't as how's I'm not appreciatin what ya done." She glanced at her older son. "It's how's I know they'd a done their meanness an gone on. Now as how they's riled up good, they's gonna git their friends an come back fer vengeance."

The boys knew she was right.

"We can beat them, Ma," Thomas beamed at Duane.

"Yer ma's right," the older boy spoke. "We kin take on two 'r three, an may be even four. But they'll come on, more 'n likely, with a scoutin patrol 'r could be a company lookin fer a bivouac."

"Come an set," the woman offered as she steered the youngsters toward the table and benches near the cook stove. "We'll meet yer friend, Thomas, an think on what needs doin."

"You a real soldier?"

"Did ya ever be in a fight?"

"Ya see any dead Yanks?"

The children lost their shyness and bubbled with curious questions.

"I seen fightin," Duane responded. "There's lots a killin an hurtin. It ain't nice nohow."

19

Thomas laid his rifle across the table and sat on a bench across from his hero. "I was gonna fight, too. But Ma won't allow it."

"She's right, ya know."

"But I wanta help kill Yanks! Ain't that what it's all about? You kill any Yanks, Dee?"

"Yes, I've killed. But it's all wrong. They's people, too. Some is real fine folk." His voice broke at the thought of his lost friends. "Some as even saved ma life."

The small group talked on while the woman fixed some hot broth, flavored with some old bones left from a small rabbit eaten days ago. Eventually the conversation returned to the dilemma at hand.

Duane offered a suggestion. "If'n Thomas was ta hide his gun out back an I was ta head on out the lane, ya could say as how a lone Reb come on when the Yanks was here and started shootin. Ya show em ma tracks an may be they'd set off ta git me an leave ya's all be." He glanced at the woman.

"Well, Ma?" Thomas asked impatiently when she sat in silence.

"Could be, Dee. But what of you?" She stood near the table, absentmindedly wiping her hands on her apron.

"I'm fixin ta take the fork ta Tullahoma an ketch up ta Bragg's army."

"But that's west a here by mor'n a mile!" Thomas cut in.

"What?"

"Yeh, we's passed that on the run from the Yanks."

No one spoke for a full minute.

"Thet does put thin's in a bit of a fix," the woman began. "But there's a rail stop on east at Manchester an I think it's open jest now ta git ta Tullahoma."

"I best git on then," Duane stated. "Ain't a whole lot a time fer some 'n heads in here."

"You go bye?" one of the girls asked.

"Guess thet be so," Duane acknowledged.

After a brief farewell, the lone boy found himself on his journey once more. He paused at the edge of the lane to turn and wave farewell to the family standing silhouetted in the open door of the farmhouse. Then, with the strengthening breeze whipping the snowdust across his face, he plodded along the lane toward the open road. Once beyond the protection of the shrub-lined path, Duane turned eastward and felt the force of the storm at his back.

* * *

Only a few minutes had passed when a rabbit darted from the underbrush. It paused in the middle of the road to stare in surprise at the boy who stood motionless so as not to frighten the creature. Duane watched admiringly as white fur moved on to blend into the snowfall. Suddenly, it occurred to the boy that something must have spooked the rabbit. He brought his musket from its resting place, butt up on his shoulder, to readiness in both hands, and reached his thumb to cock the hammer.

"Wouldn't do that, Boy," a tall bearded figure warned as he stepped from the bushes.

"Guess we told him, eh Bobby?" the fat man joined from across the roadway.

The Union troopers stepped forward from their hiding places. Each had his rifle leveled on their captive.

"Well looky here," the first continued. "If it ain't a little Johnny Reb." He reached out and removed the gun from the boy's grasp. "Wonder if he knows how we come to be shot at a while back?"

"Yeh," the raspy voice added. "Could be we should show him some respect for his elders."

Fear knotted in the pit of his stomach as Duane assumed they might decide to shoot him where he stood and let the snowfall bury him.

"Ya figger ta be real brave bein yer two agin me," his voice quavered. "Ya be . . ."

A rifle butt slammed against the side of his face, sending him spinning to the ground. He had seen it coming and stepped to

21

avoid the blow, but wasn't fast enough. Still, it saved him from loosing any teeth, suffering instead, a bloody mouth. The boy lay motionless in the snow, conscious, but unwilling to let his captors know. He tasted the warm flow as his blood seeped from the cuts in his tongue and the inside of his cheek. Relaxing his jaw and letting his whole body lay limp, he permitted it to slip from his lips and pool on the white snow.

"Now look what you did!" the fat soldier called angrily. "You've gone and killed him. He ain't no use dead!"

Thank goodness for that, Duane thought.

"He ain't dead," the bearded man returned. "You get the horses. We'll heave him across my saddle and take him back for the captain. He'll probably want him for a trade along the way."

Duane shivered involuntarily as the cold stung his face.

"See," the smaller man affirmed, "he's still alive."

The horses were retrieved from their place of concealment. Duane was laid across the saddle, gear and all. The troopers mounted, the lighter one riding the rump of his horse behind the saddle. They turned back the way they had come and rode westward, into the storm.

*　　*　　*

In the days ahead, Duane found himself captive of a small company of marauding Federal cavalry. Led by a puritanic contradiction of a captain, the company traveled steadily eastward on a scouting mission to gather information concerning Confederate strength in Eastern Tennessee, particularly around Knoxville.

Captain Terence Bartell was the model of Christian charity with his own men and people he knew. At the same time, he was just as quick to put strangers to the sword and property to the torch. A small man, only five foot seven, he walked and rode rigidly erect.

It was the heavy trooper with the deep rasping voice, Brandon Yardley, who first saved Duane's life. Upon their arrival in camp, Bobby wanted to do the killing and the captain was most agreeable. But Brandon, a corporal by rank, suggested the boy might come in handy as a trade-off in a tight spot, reminding his friend at the same time that the idea was originally his. Captain Bartell concurred and Duane become a prisoner of war.

For three days the small company of a score of men moved through the country roads, skirting Sparta and Crossville in route. Just east of Crossville, the company spied a wagon of Confederate wounded on the road. The captain called a halt.

After a brief meeting with his junior officers, he announced to his men, "We're gonna take them. The Lord has said an eye for an eye and a tooth for a tooth. So also is it a life for a life." There was a murmur of approval as he concluded. "There'll be no prisoners."

"I'll keep an eye on the boy," Brandon offered.

"Okay," the captain accepted. "But come up as soon as we're done."

"Yes, Sir."

The captain drew his saber, held it over his head, then silently lowered it forward. Breaking into an open run, the company charged the wagon. Duane watched the slaughter in helpless horror. Screams of agony rent the air. The boy noticed that Brandon, too, shuddered silently as he looked on. No shots were fired. The bloody work was done with saber.

"They needn't a done thet," Duane sobbed.

"I know," Brandon agreed. "But this war's made crazy men of them."

The corporal led the boy to join the company, already at work scavenging the corpses and loading their booty into the wagon. Leaving the bodies in the blood-splattered snow, the troopers took the wagon and continued on their way.

Snowfall had ended the previous day. Grey weather had set in and darkness gathered early. The company left the road and made camp for the night in a small hollow, hidden in a forested hillside. A hot meal was prepared from the supplies found in the wagon, then all settled in for a cold night's sleep. Duane was tied to the wagon's wheel by a lead rope from his bound hands. Brandon found some extra clothing from the wagon for him to sleep on and covered him with an extra horse blanket. The boy slept fitfully, tossing and turning in his attempt to ease the discomfort in his wrists, and somehow passed a very painful night.

Shortly after dawn, all hell broke loose. Corporal Yardley had untied the boy and seen to his breakfast of cold biscuits and coffee. The two stood near the fire as the captain approached. He was about to pass when Duane spoke out.

"Ya shouldn't a kilt them wounded, Captain. It ain't being the Christian man ya calls yerself." It was simply a statement of his feelings, made in frustration. He was helpless to do any more.

"I'm beginning to take a liking to you, Boy." He stopped to face the boy, folding his arms across his chest in pious patience. "But your kind of young to pass opinion. You ever shot a Yank?"

"Yes, Sir, Yank and Rebel both. I ain't fer bein kilt and I've shot many of a mind ta do me in."

Surprise registered on the captain's face. "You telling me you've been in battle?"

"With Breckinridge at Shiloh and Sheridan at Perryville and Murfreesboro."

"That can't be. One's of the Confederate Army and the other's of the Union!?" He shifted his stance placing his hands on his hips as he gazed into the boy's eyes to judge the truth of his statement.

Duane returned a steady look as their eyes met and the officer suddenly realized the boy was not lying.

"I ain't here takin sides in this fightin. It jest . . ."

A volley of gunfire erupted from the trees all around the clearing. The hail of lead sliced through the company like a storm through a wheat field. The captain grabbed the boy, spinning him by the arm, as he folded Duane in a protective hug and fell forward into the snow. The impact of a dozen bullets blew the corporal off his feet and threw him backwards onto the ground. The roar of continuous rifle and revolver firepower lasted for about three minutes as the Confederate force advanced from their cover to make sure there were no survivors.

"Don't move," the captain instructed as he fell on the boy, impressing his body into the foot-deep snow covering on the ground. His overcoat flew open as they went down and completely concealed the young figure beneath the man. "Wait till they've gone before you even stir a muscle or you're dead for sure."

The voice faltered as the dying man choked on his own blood, rushing forth from shattered lungs.

Duane endured the weight on top of him as a memory flashed through his mind of a distant battle and a friend who had shielded his body from death. He concentrated on remaining motionless and listened intently as the gunfire ended, hoping to hear the definite departure of the troops who had ambushed the company. All he heard was silence.

A single gunshot shattered the quiet. Someone was checking.

Silence.

Duane ached in his attempt to remain motionless. The cold damp of the melting snow soaked his clothing and chilled his body. He felt a sticky dampness seeping through the snow above his head and cramped hands. Still he lay unflinching. The silence stretched into an eternity. The boy became groggy and drifted into sleep.

An hour passed before he awoke with a start. His body was becoming numbed by the cold. He tried to move and found the weight on his back had stiffened with the cold and death.

It must be safe, now, Duane thought to himself. He pushed himself up and with some difficulty, rolled the captain's body aside. The impression in the snow where he had lain was pooled with blood. It was the blood he had sensed earlier. It was on his hands and in his hair, and covered the clothing on his back.

Duane shuddered at the litter of bloody bodies scattered about in the snow, shattered by a hundred bullets. He guessed the horses were spared. They were gone. Everything else remained.

Sensing a deep coldness within, the boy glanced toward the sky. Overcast had moved in. More snow was on the way. It was time to move on.

The captain's bullet-riddled coat was spared the blood bath, having remained spread across them both. Duane worked to remove it from the stiffening corpse, to have it for extra warmth on his journey. Gathering up his gear, he stripped off his own bloody coat and hat, wiping the blood from his hands and head on the inside surface of the garment before discarding it in the snow. Then he pulled on the great blue overcoat. Lifting his pack to his back, the boy headed off into the hills.

Duane had heard that the road ran east across the river to Kingston, then on to a railroad and connections to the army. He would cut through the hills and mountain country to avoid the possible danger of a run-in with renegade cavalry which could prove dangerous.

The boy wandered for two days in desolate mountain country, desperately aware that he had become lost. His provisions ran out to some cold hardtack and dried salt pork. The overcast had hung on with an occasional wet mist, but no storm developed. Night came, and Duane found shelter in a shallow cave. Dragging in a pile of dead branches, he broke them into kindling, lit a fire for warmth, ate the last of his food, and settled into a fitful sleep.

* * *

The coals glowed with a silent foreboding, disturbed occasionally by a flurry of cold snow born into the cave by the night breeze. A hiss of defiance greeted the flakes in their attempts to smother the warmth of the waning fire. A rustling movement intruded on the silent battle between heat and cold. The coals winked. Again the rustling movement. The damp black walls shivered. There echoed a splat as a drop of moisture fell from them onto a rock and slowly solidified into a slick solid. Fewer flakes were met with the haughty hiss. The embers were dying. The cold stealthily slipped in. Again the rustling movement, this time accompanied by a slow sigh of air. Silence. A splat. A hiss. Silence. Silence.

A startled movement shocked the stillness. Duane, shaking violently in the grip of the damp cold, sat up and dragged himself closer to the faint red glow. Shivering hands reached into the blackness in search of wood pieces. Placing the wood over the few remaining embers, he breathed with a halting steadiness on the red glow until a flickering of life appeared. Encouraged, he blew harder and the flames grew merrily to attack and to drive back the cold.

Dancing flames brightened the grim rock with prancing shadows and silhouettes. The boy rubbed his sleepy eyes with the heels of his hands and pushed back the dark tangle of hair. Stretching and shaking, he drew his blankets tightly about his wornly clothed, chilled self, and hunched close to the fire. The weight of constant travel pulled at his eyelids.

The morning breeze stung him on the face with a white flurry. Duane gazed beyond the fire. A sudden fear gripped him as he realized the need to find shelter, food, and warmth; or he would die. His food supply had just run out and he had wood for a few hours only. Now the snow made it necessary that he find a camp or a settlement, somebody, or else freeze to death.

As these thoughts ran through his consciousness, he reached for his gear. He pulled on the oversized blue overcoat and slung his pack over his shoulders. With the overcoat securely tied and the blankets folded and worn cloak-fashion, the boy left the glowing red warmth of the fire for the steady fury of the white cold and the deathly silent, smoothly blanketed world of snow.

He paused momentarily at the opening of the cave. Behind him burned the fire. In front lay a wilderness he'd never before seen, and the bludgeoning of a growing storm. Since the army lay in the east he would head in that direction. He stepped forward and melted into the snowy silence.

As Duane knew from the position of the last twilight the previous day that the cave faced to the southeast, he was able to take his bearings from it upon beginning the journey and head due east. But once away from it, he gradually lost all sense of direction. Everywhere there were trees and everywhere the trees were padded with white on the skyward surfaces. And all was encased in the silent swish of the white among the dark gnarled limbs, naked except for the padded surfaces.

The wilderness seemed to hold its breath and to watch in wonder as the boy pushed on, for not a breeze stirred; only the silent swish of the white prevailed. Traveling was not difficult at first; only a few inches of snow had fallen. But by full daylight, a hint of motion began to swirl in the air.

The boy did not know when the moment of daybreak had arrived or how much of the day had passed since that moment. He did not know how long he had been traveling or even if he were traveling in the right direction. He did realize that he was tiring, the snow was deepening and falling more thickly, and he could no longer see very far ahead before his gaze was lost in the white blaze. The boy stumbled and went down on his knees, but the reflex bracing of his arms and hands kept him from falling any further.

Duane suddenly realized that he must have dozed while walking, and the thought scared him. Washing his face with the cold white powder, he forced himself to his feet and moved on. The deafening silence swished about endlessly and the boy felt it squeeze him in its grip. A grumbling stomach growled for food. Aching muscles begged for rest. Burning eyes pulled for darkness. Visions of a soft bed by a fire danced on the weary mind. And snow stung the burning face.

Pausing, Duane brushed his coat sleeve-covered hand across his snow-wet face, then surveyed his surroundings. Where the branches forked on the trees, he could see foot-high drifts of white powdered dampness. The boy was caught in a sphere of white broken only by the dark undersides of tree branches. He moved on, but he could no longer sense any movement on his own part, only the motion of dark branches passing over his head. His ears roared with the swishing silence. He felt a tenseness surge through his body and a damp chill run up his back. He was afraid.

Suddenly he felt himself sliding swiftly downhill and momentarily everything became a blur. When all movement stopped and the boy felt the security of stillness, he looked about himself and discovered that he was sitting on ice. He moved to regain his feet and heard a resounding pop followed by the swishing stillness. He froze in mid motion. Trying once again, the silence was shattered by an ear-splitting explosion and Duane felt a foot fall away underneath him and felt a sensation of warmth as his foot plunged through ice and into icy water. Fighting panic, he carefully pulled the leg out of the water and back onto the ice. Then, with deliberately slow movements he inched his way to the banks of the river only to find that the embankments were too steep to climb. He saw where he had slid down and found his blankets in the snow at the edge of the ice. The boy was shaking with fear as he stood up and adjusted the blankets on his shoulders. The wind had been picking up for some time and was beginning to whip the snow into great clouds of white mist. Duane moved along the edge of the ice hoping to find a place to climb out onto the high ground. The soaked pant leg stiffened and froze solid and the boy was forced to limp along, unable to move the leg. A gust of wind buffeted him and he spun, staggering to hold his balance, then slipped and fell on the ice. He struggled to get up, slipped and fell again. The leg wouldn't obey. It couldn't. The boy screamed in fear, but the winds drowned out his cries. He thrashed wildly about like a deer felled, with a broken leg, trying vainly to accomplish what he knew he could not. Gradually he quieted down and sat there staring blankly at the steep slope. He slumped forward and lay limply on the ice. The wind wailed and the whipped snow drifted about the dark form on the ice.

*   *   *

Vaguely conscious of a warm dampness against his face, the boy opened his eyes briefly and perceived a dog licking at his near frozen flesh. There was a pair of moccasined feet beside the dog, and two hands reached down toward him. The boy felt a hazy sense of motion as though some almighty force were pulling him upward. He made no resistance, but slipped into the eternity of unconscious sleep.

A sweet sensation of warmth seeped in to embrace the boy's subconscious. He had no feeling of contact with anything, nor could he feel the presence of his own body. Deathlike numbness blanketed his mind. Gradually he became aware of a surrounding warmth, then the smell of smoke and of something which might be food. He sensed the crackling sound of a small fire and became aware of his own presence and of pressure on his body.

The boy, stripped of his wet clothing, lay on a bed of animal skins and was covered with a large, black, bear skin blanket. His clothing hung near the fire on a crude rack made of branches and rawhide. An occasional hiss mixed with the crackling of the fire as melting snow dropped from the clothing and onto the fire-heated rocks that corralled the flames. There was a temporary splash of running water as an Indian girl rung out a damp cloth and bent over the boy to bathe his frostbitten hands and face.

The fire's light illuminated the interior of an Indian dwelling built of branches and a mud plaster. Along one end wall stood some earthen jars and reed baskets along with the family's personal possessions. Animal skin beds on low frames of oak or ash wood splints lined the other end wall. A hide hung over the doorway to keep out the snow and weather. A small hole in the roof of the dwelling allowed the fire's smoke to escape. Beside the fire, a large earthen pot of broth simmered on the heated rocks.

Feeling a sudden coolness in the air, the Indian girl turned toward the door as the hide was pushed aside and a young man clad in a snow-blanketed, skin robe entered the lodge. A small mongrel dog following at his heels stopped just inside the doorway to shake off the fresh snow, revealing a well-brushed, dust-yellow coat. The man removed his robe, shook the snow from it, and hung it on a tripod beside the door opening. His long black hair glistened from melted snow. Sweat streaked the smooth brown skin of his face and bare arms. Outside the dwelling stood a fresh supply of wood which he had been gathering.

The woman quickly left the boy and filled a wooden bowl with broth which she served to the man standing there. Draining the contents of the bowl, he set it by the pot and went over to the boy. The dog had already settled on the furs at the boy's feet. Duane's face was turned toward the fire, and in the firelight it looked very pale. His arms lay limply on the furs at either side. No sign of motion was evident—not even a slight rise and fall of his chest. The man asked his wife if there had been any change. She shook her head.

Kneeling beside the bed, the Indian gently passed his hand over the boy's face and arms and found the flesh cold and dry. Leaving him momentarily, the man went over to a corner in the lodge and rummaged around until he found an old army blanket. With the help of his wife, he rolled Duane over, spread the blanket, then lay him back on it. Turning the bearskin down, the Indian began a long slow process of bathing the boy with slightly warmed water. After a while he heated the water until it was tepid and again bathed the body. For nearly an hour he continued, increasing the water temperature by slow steps, until the cold flesh began to take on some color and show some sign of life. He spoke to the woman and then walked over to the fire and warmed his hands. She dried Duane off, recovered him with the warm skin blanket, then went for some wood to build up the fire.

31

With new warmth in the air, the Indian returned to the bed, removed the wet blanket, and handed it to the girl who hung it near the fire to dry. Having wrapped the bear skin snugly about the child, he turned to his own bed and lay down for the night. The girl banked the fire, put a few things away, then she, too, turned in. The dog maintained his place at Duane's feet.

Even though he had been vaguely aware of all that had happened during the past hours, Duane had been unable to move or to think about moving any part of his body. He felt suspended in a void unable to react in any way to his surroundings. He couldn't even breathe, though the air seemed to flow in and out of his lungs without any effort on his part.

The night passed quietly and the following day dawned bright and sunny. Brilliant rays of sunlight streamed into the lodge illuminating the dust in the streaked pattern which they created. The girl was bustling about preparing a breakfast, but the Indian was already gone. It was mid-morning when he returned with two rabbits—skinned, cleaned, and ready for cooking. Hanging them on the outside of the lodge, he entered and hung his robe on the tripod. The dog entered at his heels, shook off the snow, and trotted over to check on the boy. The dog's whines brought the couple to the bedside. Leaning closer, the Indian saw that the boy was breathing more deeply.

Duane felt a damp nose on his face and stirred slightly to turn away from it. Next he felt a tongue licking at his cheek and reached up to find out what it was and to push it away. Suddenly he was aware of the close presence of people and of the noise of the fire and of the dog licking his face and of the sunlight streaming into the dwelling. He opened his eyes and winced at the brightness. He saw the brown-skinned faces and tried to relate them to his existence and could not figure out how they fit. Duane opened his mouth to speak, but nothing would come out. The pretty girl looking at him placed her finger to his lips as if to signal silence, so he ceased his effort to talk and smiled instead. The man smiled back and pointed to his stomach to ask if Duane was hungry. The boy nodded weakly and the girl dipped out a bowl of broth.

As he ate, a youth entered the lodge and spoke quietly to the older man. Duane guessed him to be a year or two older, but wasn't sure. His clothing was a mix of crude home-spun fabric and a factory-loomed cloth. He stood a few inches taller than Duane and was of a slender build with long black hair hanging freely across his shoulders. The youth approached the patient and sat on the dirt floor next to the bedding.

"Hello," he greeted.

"Ya kin talk?" Duane returned.

"Some," he replied in a strong voice. "I am called Eqwani Stetsi, or River Child, because I was born in a boat while my mother traveled the river."

"I'm Dee," Duane introduced.

Eqwani Stetsi introduced his uncle Inali, or Black Fox, and his aunt Nunda Dayi, or Moon Beaver. "You are from the great war across the land?" he continued. "You wear the clothing of a soldier."

"I'm lookin fer the army of the Confederacy," Duane confirmed.

"If you talk of the army with clothes the color of yours, you wear both. Which one do you seek, the coat or the shirt?"

"The shirt."

"Your army is many days journey toward the morning sun. But horse of the iron trail goes there."

"Who ar you, Ak . . . a . . . ni?"

"Eqwani Stetsi," he helped. "We are of the Cherokee Nation. We hide in these mountains where your people can't find us to follow the trail of tears."

"Then why fer ya he'pin me?"

"My uncle saw you needed help." The reply was simple, and accompanied by nodded agreement from the man and the girl who stood nearby, watching with interest the conversation of the two boys of different worlds. "He was on a hunt," the Indian boy continued, "when the storm struck. On the way back to the village his dog found you on the river ice."

"I sher am obligin to ya," Duane said. "Ya jest set me fer thet iron trail an I'll not be sayin nothin 'bout eve' seein ya."

The older boy and his family spoke briefly. Then Eqwani Stetsi continued, "I will guide you through the mountains when you are strong enough to travel. My uncle says to wait three days. Now eat and get strong."

*　　*　　*

The days passed quickly. In part, they were an adventure in learning of a people very new to him. In part they were a time of rest from the tenseness of the war. The peace of the mountains was a medicine all its own. It helped to heal a wounded spirit deep within the boy in affirming that there was a part of the world where beauty and peace and goodness really existed. Gladly would he have stayed in the mountains if his father were there with him.

But he wasn't. He continued to be lost in the war which was now so far away. Even as he walked the snowy beauty of the winter forest and watched the living creatures in their daily wanderings, he knew he had to go.

The third day found the boy fully healed as Inali had said he would be. Duane gathered together his gear and packed to leave. Nunda Dayi prepared some extra dried venison and fried bread for the journey. In appreciation, Duane offered his rifle and all its ammunition to Inali. He figured that he had the revolver which would serve him well. The gift was accepted with honored pride and carefully placed on the far wall of the dwelling.

Duane left the warmth of the lodge for the journey through the mountains with Eqwani Stetsi. The man and his woman stood before their home with all their relatives to wave the boys off on a safe journey.

The sun was bright. The air was crisp and clear. The boy was refreshed and enthusiastic as the two left the home place and headed into the wilderness.

Were the two able to travel in a straight line toward the rail line, the journey would have been about twenty-five miles. As it was, the mountainous terrain stretched the distance to about thirty-six rugged miles. To make matters worse, the weather shifted quickly as fog settled in about dusk of the first day, only to give way to rain. Torrential rains hampered travel throughout the second day. Finally, late in the afternoon of the second day, the two were able to gaze from the wooded slopes to view a narrow valley and its fragile ribbon of railroad, barely visible through the soaking mist during a brief letup in the stormy weather.

"Here I say good-bye," the Cherokee youth stated as he stood, drenched by the day's travel. "You will have a safe journey. I cannot go further with you and be safe."

"Are ya safe ta git back home?" Duane asked. He shook the water from his hat and returned it to his rain-soaked head.

"I know this country well," Eqwani Stetsi replied. "Many days to the east, many of my people live on lands a good white man bought for them. There are also many of my people still hiding in these mountains. I will journey first to a place I know near here. There I can rest by a warm dry fire. Then I'll go home. You see where the valley grows narrow toward the south?" he pointed and Duane nodded an acknowledgment. "There you will find a place called Sweet Water. Your people there can help you find your army and maybe a dry place for the night."

"I sher do thank ya. An I hope yer people do okay." Duane extended his hand.

The older youth accepted the hand in friendship. Quietly they shook, smiled at each other, then parted. As Duane began to work his way toward the valley floor, his guide watched briefly his progress. But after a hundred yards of travel, the boy looked back and his friend was gone.

*　　*　　*

Sweet Water proved a welcome stop. A young storekeeper and his sister gave Duane a place to sleep the night and spend a dry day. The boy learned the main army, which was under the leadership of General Robert E. Lee, lay encamped nearly five hundred miles to the northeast. Duane wondered if he might work his way back toward Tullahoma. To this idea, the storekeeper explained that such a trip was very dangerous and not likely to succeed due to Union Cavalry activity throughout eastern Tennessee. The safe, sure way to get to the army was to join Lee in northern Virginia.

So it was that Duane began his journey into Virginia the following morning. The storekeeper secured passage on the Virginia and Tennessee Railroad most of the way. Due to the rainy weather and war conditions, the trip could take several days and require changes in route. Duane didn't care. He was happy to be dry and warm, and to know he would soon be on his way again.

The journey from Sweet Water began with two more days of rain. After five days of travel and delay, the boy arrived at Orange Court House in northern Virginia. By the time he arrived there, the weather had turned once more to snow.

From Orange Court House, the boy took the road east toward Fredericksburg and the encampments of the Army of Northern Virginia.

*　　*　　*

The morning of the second day was beautifully sunny. Duane had traveled constantly from the rail stop, so that he could cover the thirty miles as quickly as possible. It was slow going in the deep snow, so he stayed to the road as much as possible. Traffic was light, a local youngster afoot or someone riding horseback on an errand. Once, a horse-drawn sleigh went past, but it was headed in the wrong direction.

Somewhere in the distance, the air reverberated with the Rebel yell. Hundreds of soldiers were charging an enemy. The boy stopped to listen. Air currents must be playing tricks, he thought. He couldn't hear the sound of battle. The musket, rifle, and cannon fire were missing. Duane hurried on, walking briskly, too tired to run.

New sounds drifted on the air—the long roll beat of the drum and the call of bugles assembling their troops. They weren't that far away. The smell of the smoke of hundreds of cook fires drifted strong on the morning breeze. Yet still the sound of battle was absent.

Cresting the rise in the road, Duane gazed down more than a mile of open valley, flanked along both sides with thousands of tents and rough-cut log cabins, gathered about a maze of company streets. At a glance, the valley appeared to hold the better part of a division's camp. The hills bore acres of tree stumps from which the logs had been cut for winter quarters. Further back were thick stands of red oak and pine woodland.

There it was that the battle was unfolding. A mass of many hundreds of troops in line of battle with flags and banners flying in the breeze, was in hot pursuit of another, smaller, troop line in slow retreat. Wild yelling from a thousand throats echoed about the valley as the soldiers fired upon one another with volley upon volley of snowballs.

Duane watched in disbelief. It was a scene of madness, so inviting in its humor and great fun. But he was too exhausted to rush forth into the fray, and chose instead to find a snow-covered rock outcrop which would serve as a vantage point for spectating.

As the rampage moved sluggishly up the valley, fresh troops joined the action. A line of reinforcements, nearly a mile long, all in orderly companies with banners slapping in the breeze, arranged itself along the nearer hills and began to advance. In the distant camp, more regiments prepared to enter in support of their retreating comrades. Duane stared in awe as the conflict swelled to nearly ten thousand soldiers, all letting loose a barrage of snowballs or rushing to seize members of the opposition as prisoners. The reinforcements clashed in one great mass of humanity and flying snow.

Unexpectedly, a flash of white fabric was hoisted high on a fence rail, and the entire conflict gradually ceased as many companies, believing a surrender to have occurred, began to drift back to their camps. The great snowball battle ended. The valley lay littered with hats, torn clothing, discarded packs, and a few wounded soldiers, scattered about the torn-up snowscape.

As Duane prepared to enter the army's camps, he became aware of another who had been watching nearby. A Negro youth approached the boy.

"Mass'r, yuz don wanna go in ther," he warned. "They's a bunch a crazy men from Texas an' Georgia." He shifted the weight of a sack slung over his shoulders. "Ya come with me, Mass'r, 'n I'll put ya up with real fightin soldiers from Alabama."

"An how fer might thet be?" Duane asked.

"No mor'n three miles south an east a here," the young slave replied.

"Why fer ya so fer out?" the boy inquired.

"When yuz gonna pick up sum extra vittles, ya's not wantin ta take from yer closer neighbors." He pointed to the sack.

"Oh," Duane acknowledged. "Who are ya eny ways?"

"Call me Willis. I'm Willis Rogers on account as I'm Captain Zachery Rogers' personal boy."

"Call me Dee."

Duane rose from his seat and stretched tired muscles as he studied the young servant. He seemed in his late teens. His black hair was in tight curls, close to his scalp. His skin was a rich brown in color, where it showed through the bundle of thread-bare clothing.

As the two started on their way, Duane noticed the tracks in the snow. Willis had followed him to his vantage point having come across the open fields from a distant farm, then turned up from a swale in the snowscape that seemed to indicate a buried roadway. The two returned to the roadway which the black youth seemed to know well, then journeyed across country to the camp of which he'd spoken.

Conversation along the way provided an opportunity for introductions between the two and news of the war from their differing experiences. The boy learned they were almost two miles south of Fredericksburg with Confederate troop camps in a semicircle from the riverbank on the north to the riverbank on the south. The Union Army was encamped across the river. It was half again as large as Lee's. Yet the two armies had fought to a standstill some seven weeks back, with heavy losses on both sides. The battle had unfolded in and around the city of Fredericksburg from which the Federal troops had withdrawn to the opposite banks of the Rappahannock River. The two armies were now in winter camp. A mutual truce had settled throughout the region as the common soldiers had declared a temporary end to hostilities and were busily engaged in commerce through whatever means the imagination could devise.

Willis explained that Company K was from a small town called Bell's Tavern, in the northern wilds of Alabama. The nearest place of any size was Elyton, about 20 miles due east. Company K was part of the 13th Alabama under Colonel Brickett D. Fry. Their camp lay to the south of the Texans by two miles or more. Along the way, Duane realized that he and his companion were skirting the outer camps of an immense army. More than 60,000 troops sprawled about the stretch of camps of the various divisions of the Army of Northern Virginia.

Having already passed through a number of camps along the way, the two finally entered the area inhabited by the regiments of General Archer's brigade. The area was quite open with many acres of orderly company streets, lined with rows of tents and crude log structures by varying degrees. Many log walls were roofed with canvass. A very few had wooden roofs. Some structures, log and canvass tent, had chimneys added at one end, created from long saplings stood upright and packed with mud.

39

The camps were packed close to one another so that a single acre might hold close to three hundred soldiers or the better part of a regiment.

The air was thick with the noise of an active outdoor community of thousands of men and beasts. It was thick, too, with the odors of such a gathering from fire smoke, to coffee, to food, to unwashed bodies and clothing, to refuse, to latrine trenches, to rotting straw. Duane felt the thickness close in on him as he traveled the camps and arrived at his temporary destination. In spite of the camp's desperate appearance, it was fairly clean and orderly. Some of the infantrymen were busy washing their laundry in large wooden tubs. Others had shared the tubs earlier. Their wash hung across lines which had been strung between tents.

"Whar's Cap'n Rogers, Mass'r Foley?" Willis asked a 19-year-old private, busy at his wash tub.

"If'n I was a bettin man, which ya know's I ain't, I'd say as ya'd find him with Lieutenant Guthries, Willis." The young private paused to wring out a wet pair of socks, then lay them across the wooden rim while he searched the sudsy water for his johns. "Ya know how fond they are of cards. They kin smell the promise enywhere's in camp."

"Ol' Sarg about?" Willis substituted.

"In his house."

The private bent back to his work.

"Come on, Mass'r Dee. I'll lead ya on ta meet Ol' Sarg Raymond. He's 'bout the oldest man in the company."

The company's quarters were a line of canvass tents with side walls about three feet high. At the officers' end were some stranger quarters with log walls. One even had a door frame, complete with solid oak door, built into the front end and a stove pipe protruding from the back.

Smoke drifted from the chimney pipe and the front door stood ajar. It looked dark inside as Duane and Willis approached the dwelling.

The black youth tapped on the door frame.

"Mass'r Sarg. Mine's if I's come in?"

"Come on, Willis," a firm voice answered. "Ya know it's open."

The two entered to find the man stretched on his bed, reading a volume of Mark Twain. Shifting to a sitting position, he lay the book on the makeshift table created from a cracker crate stood on end.

"Who's yer friend?" the sergeant asked.

"This here's Mass'r Dee," Willis introduced. "I picked him up near ta Hood's camp. We was watchin them blame fool Texans a sno-fightin them Georgia fools."

The sergeant seemed friendly enough. He was strict-looking with his dark eyes and deep brown hair. His full beard with its two stripes of white added to his firmness, and was enough to remind people of a skunk. Duane smiled to himself, but made sure his face gave no hint of the humor he'd observed.

"Fetch us up some vittles, Willis," Raymond ordered. "Dee here must surely stand in need of nourishin."

"Yes, Mass'r Sarg, Sir." The servant turned and left.

"Sit down, Dee," the sergeant continued. "There's a rations box by my trunk ya kin pull up."

Duane pulled out the box and settled in the middle of the floor. Dropping his gear on the packed dirt floor at his side, he peeled off the overcoat and enjoyed the warm feeling of the heat radiating from the small coal stove. The two visited for almost an hour. Willis brought a plate of beans with some scraps of salt beef. They were still warm from the fire. Sergeant Raymond poured two tins of coffee from the pot on his stove. Duane learned the stove had been taken from a wrecked railroad coach back in the fall and packed in with the company's camp wagon. The boy shared his description of the snow battle and they both laughed at the thought of whole regiments firing snowballs back and forth. The man explained that there had been a number of smaller such engagements, but this was, by far, the grandest about which he had heard.

Duane learned some of the company's history and its membership. Many of the men were relations. It's youngest member, Tod Gardner, was its fourteen-year-old drummer boy. He had lost his older brother, Jason, in the battle in December. A cousin had been wounded and sent home earlier in the fall campaign. Three uncles were still with the company. The Jenkins family and relations had at one time made up about a sixth of the company. Tod was part of that family.

Sergeant Raymond decided that Duane's medical training and battlefield experience would make him a valuable orderly. Tod could use his company to help distract him from his grief and make him responsible for showing the new boy around. Tod's uncles, Foley and Kim, would be pleased to see him out of their tent and occupied with responsibility. So it was decided that Tod's tent would be set up where the wood yard presently stood between the officers' country and the rest of the company's quarters.

*   *   *

The days passed slowly as Duane became acquainted with his new outfit. Tod was tolerant of the new tentmate and quarters situation, but remained cool toward the outsider who had caused him to be removed from his uncles' tent. The company's routine began with morning muster, followed by breakfast, followed by drill, followed by free time, followed by noon muster, and so on throughout the day. On some afternoons, the whole regiment would drill together. Regimental muster took place each evening and was usually reviewed by the balding Colonel Brickett D. Fry.

Duane felt a growing sense of loneliness. His only friendly acquaintance was the houseboy, Willis. The black youth had become quite protective of the company's newest and youngest member, and sought to help him out of his sadness.

Early one morning during the first week after Duane's arrival, he and Tod were awakened by Willis in his usual duty to rouse the drummer for muster. As the two sat in their cots, rubbing sleep from their eyes, the older youngster decided to sleep in.

"Hear'd tell ya was a drummer," he began sleepily.

"Thet be true."

"Thet bein the case, may be ya'd spell me jest now and I'd git back ta dreamin." Tod dropped back on his bed and pulled the blankets up over his head as he shivered in the freezing cold.

"I'd be pleased ta stand in fer ya." Duane pushed off the covers, shaking uncontrollably in the cold air, then moved quickly to pull on his clothing which he had taken to bed. It was still warm from being slept upon. "Ya sure, Tod, ya be wantin me ta do fer ya?" He reached for his blue overcoat and his scarf.

"Yeh fer certain. Too cold fer drummin," the muffled voice confirmed.

Duane pulled on his cold boots, jammed his hat on his rumpled head, secured the drum strap over his coat, then reached for the drum and sticks. Sliding the sticks under the strap, he tightened the drum with its leather pull tabs, hooked it to the strap, and left the tent.

Outside in the early dimness of the new dawn, Duane positioned himself and beat the mustering roll. It had been a long time and he was really out of practice. The drum roll was embarrassingly rough.

Kim and Foley Jenkins were among the first to gather.

"Whar's my nephew this fine hour?" Kim asked, his voice hoarse with a winter cough.

"In bed, I'll wager," his cousin, Foley, commented.

"Thet so?" Kim looked to Duane.

"Thet's so," Duane replied.

"Well, Cuz, let's roust him out," Kim suggested, a mischievous smile wrinkling his face.

The two disappeared into the tent which immediately erupted into loud cries of protest.

"No! No! It's too cold! Oww!"

A triumphant pair emerged from the tent bearing a struggling nephew, clad in his johns.

"No one gits ta miss fu'st muster. Right, Cuz?" Kim smiled.

"Right, Cuz," Foley grinned in agreement.

As the company gathered, the Jenkins cousins plopped their nephew in line between them for safe-keeping. The sight of the blanketed boy brought laughter to the gathering and humor to the day's beginning. Lieutenant Damien Jenkins, Kim's older brother, checked out the company for attendance.

"Soldier," he mocked at the shivering blankets, "yer out a uniform."

"Lay off, Uncle Damien!" the angered boy returned.

"My, my, what harsh words ta yer superior officer," the lieutenant chided.

"I ain't voted fer ya. Jest leave me be!" The boy's voice broke as tears of anger and embarrassment slid down his cheeks.

"Thet's 'nough teasin, Boys," Captain Rogers interrupted as he approached the company for roll call and inspection.

The company came to order as the captain checked his troops and completed the mustering routine. At thirty-two, he was of sturdy build. His black beard was trimmed close to follow the curve of his jaw. He looked official and was neatly dressed in a well-worn uniform, complete with grey great coat.

Throughout the nearby camps, companies were lining up and the new day was officially underway. The musters were completed and the noisy routine of breakfast was begun. Willis travelled the camp issuing the morning rations to each mess group. Tod glared at Duane as the two worked on the fire they shared with three other tents in their mess group.

As far as he was concerned, the embarrassment he'd suffered was all Duane's doing. How rotten his luck at being saddled with such a lousy tentmate.

"Mass'r Dee," Willis interrupted as he returned from issuing rations, "Ya come's ta Cap'n Rogers' quarters afta this mornin's drillin."

"What fer ya askin?" the boy questioned.

"Ya's jest be there."

"Sure, Willis, I'll be."

Tod remained sullen throughout the morning. He said little during breakfast and did his job silently during drill. As soon as the company was dismissed, he deposited his drum in the tent and wandered off into the regimental encampment. Duane reported to the captain's tent as instructed. Willis was waiting for him and led him aside to the storage tent.

"What ya say we does some tradin?" he offered.

"Whereve' is there a place fer tradin?" the boy asked in surprise. "An what fer we got ta be traded?"

"Neve' ya mine's, Mass'r Dee." He picked up a tied flour sack from beside a pork barrel. "Yuz jest come 'long with Ol Willis an we's goin ta the rive'."

"Huh?"

"Jes' come's on. Yuz'll see."

The morning air had warmed with the rising sun. Duane and Willis journeyed through the bustling camps as they wandered just under two miles to the banks of the river. Selecting a secluded cut amidst the vegetation, the youth motioned the boy to settle on a drift log. A short time later, the two were joined by Sergeant Raymond and Corporal Cameron Doherty.

"Ya bring yer supplies?" the sergeant asked.

"Right here," Willis indicated the bag.

"What's happenin?" Duane inquired.

"We's what ya might call, one of the company's tradin partners," the sergeant explained.

"We gathers supplies from home an around an brings em here ta trade with the Yank's tradin' partners." Corporal Doherty described the weekly meetings that had been arranged the previous month. He had run into a couple of Yanks while exploring down river. They were out fishing. Together they had worked an agreement to put a trading raft across the river. The Yanks could get supplies of coffee and Cameron had access to tobacco.

As he spoke, he uncovered a cord line, buried under the dirt, and tied to a sapling. The line disappeared from where it stretched across the ground to where it passed beneath the surface of the water's edge.

Sergeant Raymond pulled a watch from his pocket and checked the time. "We're early," he observed.

The small group waited quietly for several minutes. Suddenly, the cord began to rise and fall in the water as some unseen force tugged slowly in the distance.

"Easy," Willis said as Cameron began to pull slowly on the line. After ten minutes, a small raft came into view. It was about three feet square, constructed with small tree limbs and store-bought heavy cord string. A sheet of paper was tacked to its middle. The sergeant read the note.

"They've five pounds of coffee, a new razor, and a pair of shoes. What do we have to offer?" The older man looked about the group.

"I has two pounds a tobacca, give 'r take a portion." Willis set the bag by the raft.

"Here's another." The corporal produced a small cloth bundle, tied up by the corners.

"I brought two pieces a chaw an a new cob pipe." The sergeant added his booty to the pile. "Shall we see if they's wantin this trade?"

Willis and Cameron nodded in agreement. Sergeant Raymond drew a pencil from his pocket and jotted their offer on the paper.

"This being so secret-like, why fer'd ya bring me along?" Duane asked while the raft made its journey.

The sergeant explained. "Willis thought ya bein' new and experienced, ya'd be good at helpin find tradin goods. Enyway, thar warn't nothin else fer ya ta be doin. An he's takin a likin to ya."

"Fine by me," Duane accepted.

The trade was agreed upon and the goods exchanged. Date and time were set for the next meeting. The raft line was buried and the area swept of tracks. Finally, the group broke up to make their return to camp.

As Duane and his companion walked the countryside, he noticed the terrible destruction from the battle. Some buildings had been pock-marked with shot or heavily damaged in part or gutted by fire. The scattered debris of battle remained about the landscape, softened by its covering of snow. Clusters of cracker box wood slabs marked the graves of hundreds who had perished. Everywhere were the camps of the living—a noisy contrast to the silent slabs with their penciled names and notes about the dead.

"Ya seen much fightin?" Duane asked as the two passed a cluster of markers alongside a broken farm house.

"The company came on afta the summer crops was put in," Willis answered. "This here's bin ar fu'st real battle. It put me in mind of the devil's own hellfire. Neve seen sech killin. Cain't find no words ta tells of it."

"I know," Duane sighed. "It conjures up my rememberins of the fightin at Murfreesboro. It's God-awful 'n ther's no sense ta it."

The two continued on in quiet thought before Duane asked, "Why is it ya all's do yer tradin so secret?"

"Ya see's, Mass'r Dee, we knows we kin trade wi d' enemy, but we daresn't git seen at it. Is okay, so long's d' officers don't sees ya doin it. Then they's gotta punish ya. 'N they's don wanna. Ya's knowin' my meanin?"

"I knows yer meanin," Duane smiled. "Ya'll divy this stuff up?"

"It's only fer 'bouts ten a us. They's nigh ta half a dozen tradin groups as use the landin. The timin's careful so's not ta set up too much traffic ta once."

The two hurried on, returning to camp in time for noon muster. Tod was not talking yet. He remained angry for the rest of the day. The coffee was divided after muster, each bringing a small tin can in which to store his share.

*   *   *

47

Days of winter drifted quietly by. Duane's friendship with Willis grew as the two shared in each day's events. It was part of the house boy's duties to pick up supplies from the regimental commissary and to run errands to the quartermaster. He was also good at scavenging the countryside for an occasional chicken or sack of corn. The boy became quite familiar with the lay of the land as they wandered about the camps of the Confederate army.

One wintery evening was particularly memorable. It had been learned that a number of regimental bands of the Federal army were gathering at the river that night. Troops from all around Fredericksburg headed for the river to hear them play. Most of the Union army was gathered as well, seating themselves on the steep hillsides overlooking the river. A hundred yards away, on the plains along the opposite banks, the Confederate soldiers gathered.

Massing themselves as one, the bands began a performance of well-known Yankee war songs. There were JOHN BROWN'S BODY and RALLY 'ROUND THE FLAG and more. Bravado gave way to sentiment and finally finished with TENTING TONIGHT.

Duane and Willis and the rest of the company had listened along with the rest of the multitude. The boy felt a pang of excitement mixed with deep sentiment and loneliness. The music had been a grand sound and a sad sound. It tore at his emotions as thoughts of home mixed with memories of war.

Somewhere in the quiet after the last piece, a Southern soldier shouted across the stillness of the river, "Now play some of ours."

Night was approaching. Blackness edged the eastern horizon. The 150,000 soldiers of the two armies remained seated and listened as the massed bands opened with DIXIE and went on with a second repertoire of Southern favorites. MY MARYLAND, THE BONNIE BLUE FLAG, and all the rest filled the air to mix with the smell of smoke from a thousand flickering fires.

Dusk deepened to darkness. The music ended. The soldiers stood to return to their camps. Then, as if an afterthought, the bands gave forth with one final song, HOME SWEET HOME. At first the gathered soldiers tried to sing along. Their voices joined with the music from the bands into one grand reverberation of song. But the voices faltered, choked off by a great sadness while tears ran unchecked down the cheeks of a hundred thousand men and boys. Buglers throughout the Union camps began their final call of the day. TAPS mingled with the last strands of HOME SWEET HOME, stirring visions of the finality of the death of war to mix with memories of home and all that had been left behind.

The song ended. The mass of humanity began to disperse as the 150,000 separated into smaller groups, going their diverse ways as they returned to their camps.

Darkness deepened. Flickering firelight danced with the stars on black ripplings of the river's surface. Silence blanketed the countryside. The armies settled to sad and pensive ponderings, and then to sleep.

*   *   *

The weeks of winter had advanced routinely toward spring. February's final week was finishing with a misty damp drizzle of several days duration. The troops had been confined to quarters. Drill had been cancelled and musters had been cut back to mid-morning and evening only.

Earlier in the week, Duane had found a treasure as he wandered an abandoned portion of the battlefield from December. Buried in the rubble of a shattered dwelling on the southern edge of the city, he had uncovered a pantry cupboard, still stocked with staples. Stuffing the pockets of his great coat, he had brought back to Willis a supply of coffee, sugar, flour, salt, and beans. The two had then returned with empty sacks to cart off more of the same along with a broken crock of butter and stale baked goods, preserved by the cold weather. Much had already been scavenged by the rodents; but, again, the winter cold had kept it to a minimum and the two human scavengers

49

simply cut away what they felt they must. Out of this bounty had come a plan.

Duane and Tod were on speaking terms, so Duane asked if he thought his Uncle Damien might want to have some fun with the gamblers of the company. Tod liked the plan and shared it with his uncle. He, in turn, was thoroughly taken by the plan and went ahead with the arrangements. Duane secured his entire stash of coffee from Willis and gave it to Tod to give to his uncle.

Most of the Jenkins relations had gathered in the lieutenant's tent. It had a well-fueled stove and plenty of room. Damien was the oldest. His brother Kimberton, Kim for short, was eleven years his junior and two years younger than cousin Folsom, known to all as Foley. Their nephew, Tod, was the youngest of the clan and half the age of the lieutenant. Damien's friend, Lieutenant Travis Guthries and the company's Captain Zachery Rogers had gained quite a reputation as gamblers. Cards was their favorite, but they were known to bet on anything, even such trivial and mundane affairs as how many weevils could be boiled from a stale biscuit.

The lieutenant's tent was crowded. All interest was focused on the four gathered about the makeshift table engrossed in a serious game of draw poker. The captain and Lieutenant Guthries were teamed against Lieutenant Jenkins and his cousin Foley. Private Matthew Guthries had come to watch his older brother play. All the Jenkins clan plus Willis and Duane were on hand to watch. The players sat around a large overturned wooden tub. The spectators perched on footlocker, camp chair, bed and boxes, or stood behind. The company gamblers had plenty of cash money and Confederate promise from weeks of card games. The Jenkins team had four pounds of coffee, a valuable rarity at the time. Coffee matched cash, thimbleful per dollar.

The quiet rain danced on canvass roof as warm flames crackled in the stove. Silent concentration filled the air, marred only by the clatter of a stove plate as an occasional chunk of wood was added to the fire, the slap of a card against the wood, or brief conversations whenever the deck was shuffled and redealt.

The game tottered back and forth for nearly two hours before falling in definite favor of the experienced duo. Finally the captain and the younger Jenkins dropped out to let the two lieutenants battle it out. Jenkins was down to his last half pound of coffee. There was a pause to shuffle the deck.

Foley excused himself. "I'm feelin a bit poorly," he stated. "My innards is creepin some. I best go lay down a bit."

The youth left. The cards were dealt. Lieutenant Jenkins slipped off his boots as his opponent passed the cards.

"My toes are cramped," he complained as he rubbed his feet, pulled up his socks, then resettled himself. Reaching beside the table for his boots, he felt for a sewing needle he knew lay nearby, passed it through his sock, and slipped it into a knot before retrieving the boots and setting them aside.

The game continued. Behind the tent, Foley peered through a small hole in the back canvass and watched the cards Lieutenant Guthries placed in his hands. With a string in hand which ran to the knot in the socks, he telegraphed the contents of Travis's hand to his older cousin by way of a predetermined code of pulls.

Over the next hour, the game turned. Lieutenant Jenkins began to win again. Eventually, he regained all his coffee and a good deal of cash. The boys began to snicker. The joke was too good. Afraid they would give it away, Kim reprimanded them.

"Quit yer noise!" he demanded. "Ya tell yer private jokes another time an don't be botherin the game."

"I cain't help it," Duane apologized. "It's jest too funny."

"Ya best leave, then," Kim suggested sharply.

"Ain't needed," Captain Rogers interjected. "Seems our luck's gone sour. It's a good time ta give it a rest."

"How 'bout one more?" Jenkins offered. "I'll lay up all the cash winnin's against equal value."

"Since yer holdin close to four thousand a my cash money, I kin only match ya with promise mixed in," Guthries remarked.

The boys watched in anticipation, trying hard to contain their laughter. Kim moved toward them to send them on their way and caught the heel of his shoe on the string. It ripped the knot from his brother's sock.

"Ow!" Damien exclaimed.

"What's wrong?" Travis asked.

Thinking quickly, the other replied, "I knocked my toe against the tub. Guess yer right. Time's come ta give it a rest."

"Well, now," Travis reconsidered. "With yer concentration broke, it jest may be a good time fer thet one last bet."

Tod noticed the needle and sock fabric where it lay on the floor. Trying to be casual he stood to stretch and moved to stand on the metal and fabric until the guests had left.

"Another time?" Jenkins hoped.

Lieutenant Guthries offered his hand to his opponent. "I surely didn't know ya was sech a poker player 'r I wouldn't a been so reckless. We'll do this agin tamorra 'n I'll git back my money."

Jenkins accepted the handshake. "Thet'll do fine so long's this weather's so bad. Next good day 'n I'll hafta fetch more firewood."

While the game was busy breaking up, Foley sneaked back to his own tent to change into a dry set of clothes. Once the gamblers, the younger Guthries, and Willis had gone, the line was hurriedly wrapped on a stick and stowed in the foot locker.

"I cain't b'lieve it! We done pulled it off!" Duane exclaimed in a checked voice.

"Keep it down," the lieutenant warned. "Jest hope fer good weather tamorra. I ain't wantin ta go through this agin. It's too strainin ta the nerves. Ya all best head off ta fixin supper."

"What ya gonna do with all thet money?" Tod asked.

"Put it away fer now. They's sure ta figger they's bin had 'n I'll wanta be able ta give it back. If the truth ne'er be learned, we'll split it when the war's ended."

"Good by me," Kim stated.

"Yeh," the boys agreed.

Duane and Tod returned with Kim to his tent. Since it had a fire with chimney, the four had been cooking supper there during the days of foul weather.

Willis brought around the evening rations and the company settled to fixing supper. Throughout the company, the game was the topic of conversation. But only five truly knew how it had been played. And they weren't telling.

*　　*　　*

Six weeks had passed since Duane's arrival in Company K. Winter had slipped into March. The weather had begun to warm. Foraging expeditions for food supplies and firewood required extended travel. Newly arrived sutlers were setting up camp near the various army camps to sell whatever they could in food and comforts. Others had a long-standing business, but were short on everything, causing prices to rise sharply. Many of their customers had little in the way of money, only notes which promised pay. Trade between the armies was dwindling as soldiers and their officers became more cautious toward disciplinary measures. The Union Army had been reorganized by General Hooker, appointed to replace General Burnside about the time Duane was journeying toward Fredericksburg. The Confederate Army was running short on everything to the point where General Longstreet had left in February with Pickett's and Hood's divisions to forage for provisions in southern Virginia and along North Carolina's coast.

Duane, Tod, and Willis had left in search of the daily supplement of sassafras buds, wild onions, lambs quarter, and poke sprouts. These were required to help replace the lack of vegetables in the company's food supply. Meat and sugar were also in short supply. As the trio walked the countryside, passing others on their daily search, they were reminded how short they were of other things as well. The blue overcoat which Duane wore was a rare treasure. His shoes were badly worn, but they still served their purpose. There were many who had no shoes at all, only improvised wrappings of crate board and rags.

Tod's uncle had given him $50 from his bankroll in case they should find a sutler or some citizen, willing to part with anything needed by members of the company. The truth of the game had never come out, nor had a follow-up game taken place. Duties had conveniently put it off and the company's gamblers had found other interests. The winnings were used as needed for the benefit of various members of the company.

Willis had been busy traveling the camps in search of whatever. The boys had often gone along. In the process, they had become more friendly toward each other, yet an obvious resentment was occasionally evident in Tod's behavior toward Duane. Willis had explained that it was due in part to jealousy of the younger boy's experience and the hurt of his brother's death. For his part, Duane had not yet told of his personal life, especially his family. All that was known within the company was that he had no family and had gone off to war as a drummer boy from Arkansas.

The three scavengers had journeyed toward the southwest corner of the city. Along the way they had gathered enough wild onion and lambs quarter to meet their needs. Now they looked to find anything of interest in the debris from war in a broken city. Many of the homes and outbuildings had been damaged or destroyed during the fighting. Several were abandoned. Some were under repair. Some were inhabited. Activity abounded in the good weather of late winter as soldiers and citizens went about their business.

"Did ya see this part a the fightin?" Duane asked as they turned onto the dirt thoroughfare called Hanover Street.

"We was further south, Mass'r Dee," Willis answered.

Tod added, "Here was some a the bloodiest killin. See thet hill yonder?" He pointed to the high ground which rose beyond the street's end.

"Uh huh," Duane acknowledged.

"Them's Maryes Heights. Ther's a road 'cross its face, hidden b'hind thet stone wall. General Cobb's brigade held off at least six Yank charges 'cross these fields 'n yards. Back ta the rive', there was a pontoon bridge 'n the Yank army jest kept on comin ov'r from t'other side. But we jest kept cuttin 'em down on thet hillside. It was like mowin' the wheat at harvest."

As the three continued along the road, they noticed the shell-torn buildings and one barn that had been reduced to scattered debris covered by its collapsed roof structure. Rows of small mounds along the base of the slope marked the final resting places of several dozen soldiers.

"Ever' man kilt an' buried 'round the battlefield went under in his johns," Willis stated matter-of-factly.

"What fer?" Duane questioned.

"Both armies is short a clothes, 'specially shoes. 'N theys sure weren't needin 'em eny more." Willis paused to shade his eyes with his hand and scan the hillside. "Ya don't 'spose they's missed a few?" he wondered aloud.

"We could take a look," Tod offered.

"Look out!" a nearby pedestrian shouted.

A commotion spread through the motion of people as they scattered from the road ahead to get out of the way of a runaway wagon. The frightened horses tore down the roadway, stirring up a wild cloud of dust as they dragged behind an empty freight wagon with its petrified driver clinging to the seatboard. The three just barely missed being run down as they dove to the side of the road. The swirl of dust was accompanied by a child's shrieks and the pain-filled yelping of a dog. Again the motion of people flowed, this time to gather in a knot a short distance from where Duane and his friends rose to their feet and brushed the dirt from their clothes.

"Let's see what's happen'd," Tod called as he rushed toward the crowd.

The others followed close behind.

"Ya see thet!" someone exclaimed.

"Yeh," another agreed. "Thet dog could a kilt the child if the wagon hadn't a struck it down."

"He weren't doin me harm," a young girl sobbed as she knelt in the dirt by the wounded animal. "Please, somebody help my Beauty!"

No one moved.

The girl bent over a large, bloodied head. "Oh, Beauty, dear Beauty, please don't die," she whispered as tears streamed down her cheeks and choked her words. "I love ya, Beauty."

A vision of the past stole across Duane's memory. He pictured Pounder, laying bloody in the snow, having taken a bullet met for his master. The boy stared dumbly at the scene before him as tears came without warning and a tightness in his throat prevented him from speaking. He moved forward and stood beside the girl, then leaned over the dog to check its injuries.

"May be as I kin help some." Duane's voice was hoarse as he wiped aside his own tears. "Easy, Beauty," he whispered softly. "Let's see what's hurtin."

The dog was a well-bred hunter. Good care and the girl's love were evident in its grooming. This girl was also of good family. Though worn, her petticoats and dress were of quality fabric. She was ten or eleven years of age. Delicate features and long brown ringlets made the boy wonder why she was alone. She looked up at the boy's approach, her eyes wet with tears and pleading for help. Quiet apprehension settled on the crowd as Tod and Willis moved closer to watch. Cautiously, Duane lowered himself beside the dog, his soothing voice seeking to calm the animal.

"Whar's yer people, Missy?" Willis asked.

"Papa's on business," was all she said, her attention focused on the boy and her dog.

Duane stroked Beauty's head in light, gentle touches. The dog shook convulsively in fits of pain and shock. Blood flowed from her mouth and from cuts on her head and side. A leg lay grotesquely out of place, broken below the knee.

Gradually the boy's hand stroked and searched as he explored for injuries. Finally he moved to the broken leg. Suddenly, the animal cried out in pain and snapped at Duane's wrist, completely closing on it with her large, sharp teeth. Duane froze in motionless anticipation of a shattering pain which did not come. Beauty never bit down, but only touched the boy's skin lightly with her teeth. She immediately released him as a great sigh of relief escaped from the spectating crowd. The large head eased back onto the ground.

"Yer a good girl, Beauty," Duane whispered. "'N I think ya kin be fixed up good 's new."

"Annie!" a man's voice called in panic from the far side of the crowd.

"Here, Papa!" the girl responded, standing at the sound of her father's voice. "Beauty's bin hurt!"

As the girl's father worked his way through the crowd, Tod and Willis knelt in whispered conversation, asking Duane what he would do.

"How bad's it look?" Tod inquired.

"Broken leg fer certain," Duane replied. "'N I think her jaw could be broke, too. I think we kin help her."

The girl's father was a handsome man in his late thirties. She clutched at him as soon as he approached, and sobbed into his silken shirt and vest as she described the events of the past ten minutes. He listened quietly while Duane and his friends watched respectfully, and considered how to help the animal. Annie calmed down as her father assured her he would take care of things.

"I'm Mr. Hasslett," he introduced. "Thank ya fer stoppin ta look. I'll take it from here."

"'Scuse me, Sir," Duane offered. "But Beauty here ain't needin ta die. She kin be helped 'n made better."

"It's none a yer affair, Boy. Ya jest . . ."

"Please, Papa. Hear him out." Pleading eyes won her father's consent.

Now that the excitement had passed, the crowd dispersed as people went about their business and left those concerned to do what they would.

Duane explained the dog's injuries and suggested treatment. "She may always walk 'n run with a limp, but if she's truly loved, it shouldn't make no difference."

"How is it ya come by all this larnin? An' who's ta say it'd work if I was ta okay it?" Mr. Hasslett was skeptical.

"He sher knows his doins," Willis offered at risk of reprimand for speaking out of place.

"Thet's a certain," Tod broke in, sensing the black youth's reckless situation. "He's from the fightin an's bin learned real good on doctorin."

"Ain't the same," the man persisted.

"But, Papa . . ."

"Okay!" he threw up his arms in surrender. "We try."

The man brought around his buggy and all helped gently to lift Beauty onto a horse blanket in the wagon bed. Annie spread the blanket, then carefully folded it across her beloved pet.

"Climb in," Mr. Hasslett invited. "We'll drive over to the house and see what ya kin do."

The Hasslett home was once a grand plantation manor to the north of the city. Much of the help had been sold off and a few house servants and older field hands remained. They were evident about the property fixing fences and tending gardens and household chores. Mrs. Hasslett greeted the party from the door as the buggy entered the yard. She was accompanied by two younger children, a boy of about eight and a girl about seven.

Annie told of older brothers who were off fighting in the war. She also explained that her family had been prosperous in cotton and tobacco, but much of their wealth had gone to the war effort. Her Papa was very proud of his heritage and believed completely in the strength and purity of the Confederacy.

"Matthew, what's happened?" Mrs. Hasslett called at the site of strangers and of the dog in the blanket.

Reining the team to a stop, he explained, "Beauty's bin run down by a wagon 'n this boy says he kin save her." He pointed to Duane.

"What's yer name, Boy?" the woman asked.

"Duane Kinkade, M'am," he replied.

"Well ya jest tell me how I kin help ya 'n we'll see ta Beauty straight off." She smiled and Duane knew Annie's mother would see her dog got the best of care.

The porch became the operating theater as the leg was set and splinted. The jaw was checked and found to be okay except for some broken teeth. Then the cuts and scratches were bathed and covered with salves. It took an hour of slow work in an effort to keep Beauty from being upset. She seemed to sense everyone's caring and allowed herself to be treated.

"She'll need lot's a time 'n rest," Duane said when they had finished. "Bones take weeks ta mend. She may be hurtin inside an' thet'll take time fer healin, too."

"I don't know how we kin thank ya," Mrs. Hasslett stated, "but we kin certainly offer some lemonade an' sweet cake."

"Yes, M'am!" Tod accepted.

"Shoes, Mass'r Dee," Willis whispered.

"Mrs. Hasslett," Duane spoke up, "if ya has some shoes 'r coats 'r blankets, our company could sher use 'em. We got some money ta pay fer it with."

"Some sugar 'r fresh meat 'd sher be nice, too, M'am," Tod added.

There was an awkward moment as the boys wondered if they'd asked too much and the Hassletts were taken by complete surprise at the nature of their requests.

"Matt?" the woman wondered aloud.

"We kin help some," the man agreed. "How much money ya got?"

"Fifty dollars, Sir," Willis produced the money. Then he worried if he had been too quick.

"Come on in an' we'll see what kin be arranged," Mr. Hasslett invited. "I'll join ya after I see ta puttin Beauty in the

59

kitchen. Yer nigger kin help carry the dog an' I'll see he gits fed somethin, too."

*　　*　　*

Mid-afternoon brought a chill in the air as the wagon bounced along the road leading south toward the camp. Matthew Hasslett and one of his colored had loaded it with a variety of provisions from the outbuildings and from some friends' businesses along the way. There was a barrel of salt pork, some cases of staple goods, a dozen blankets, three coats, a half dozen pairs of shoes, and an assortment of used clothes. The fifty dollars was accepted as payment in full. Should Tod's uncle wish to advance another fifty, the man had offered to bring a second wagon load within three weeks.

Passing through the various camps, the wagon finally approached Company K's tent lines. Corporal Cameron Doherty looked up from the fire he was building. The noise of the approaching wagon had caught his attention.

"Hey, Tod!" Doherty waved as he stood and approached the vehicle, "where ya'all been?"

Others came from their tents or afternoon chores to investigate the odd manner of the boys' return.

"What ya got there, Tod?" Damien asked as he stepped from his tent.

The door to Sergeant Raymond's house opened as curiosity drew him from its comfort. Eventually, half the company gathered about the wagon. While Tod stepped aside to converse with his uncle about the offer for a second supply run, Willis and the Hasslett colored unloaded the wagon. The sergeant directed that all materials be placed in front of his house until the captain decided on their distribution.

"Dee," Mr. Hasslett called him aside. "This here's fer you."

He handed the boy a brown paper package.

"But, Sir . . ."

"Jest open it. Ain't a great deal, but figger'd it'd be handy."

Duane slipped the string off and opened the paper. Tod and his uncle had come up to talk business and paused to watch. The package revealed a bar of store-bought soap, a pound sack of coffee, and a new shirt.

"The shirt was my Lance's. He's only fifteen, so's should fit ya." He smiled proudly at the thought of sharing something from his family.

"I dunno what fer ya done all this. It weren't nothin what I did. But I sher thanks ya, Mr. Hasslett." He set the soap and coffee aside to open up the shirt and hold it up for size. It was large and would hang very loose. "It'll fit right finely, Sir."

"Ya take care, now," the man said. "I'll be back by ta let ya know how Beauty heals."

"Could Annie come long, too?" Duane asked.

"We'll see."

"Mr. Hasslett," Tod spoke up. "This here's my uncle, Lieutenant Jenkins."

The two men greeted each other as Tod asked Duane to show him what he'd gotten. Wandering to their tent, the boys found something warmer to wear against the evening chill. Duane found an empty sugar sack and divided the coffee, giving half to Tod. Meanwhile, the two men discussed and agreed upon a second supply purchase. As the wagon departed the camp and the officers looked over their unexpected good fortune, the various mess groups began to build their cook fires and to prepare for dinner. This meal would include extra rations from the newly arrived stores.

*   *   *

The scent and sizzle of salt pork hung with the heavy odor of wood smoke as dinner was prepared. There were flour for baking stick bread and coffee for brewing. The smells of dinner were a bouquet of fragrance.

As the group about the fire prepared dinner, Tod related the tale of the day's adventures. It was evident in his voice that he felt a sense of pride in Duane's actions. Having completed the story, he returned to a point which had puzzled him at the time.

"Dee," Tod asked, "why was ya cryin when ya first saw the dog layin there?"

Finishing the last of his dinner, Duane paused to gulp down some coffee. Setting the cup at his side, he looked straight at the other boy.

"Ya know how it was savin Annie thet got her dog hurt?"

"Yeh."

"Well, I've a dog, too. His name's Pounder. Last I saw him he was mendin from being shot ta save ma life. I ain't seen him since 'r eny a my family. Ya see, Ma was kilt afta Pa went ta the war. I left ta find him. Got close some, but ain't found him yet." He stopped, sensing a sudden silence in the gathering.

"We're real sorry," Foley broke the silence.

"But I ain't wantin fer pity," Duane returned. "It's a friend I'm wantin, like Willis been ta me."

"Guess thet's why fer ya neve' spoke a this afer?" Kim asked.

"I figger ya really ain't needin ta know. Ya's had yer own losses 'n hurts," Duane replied.

Tod said nothing. Pretending exhaustion, he rubbed his eyes and stretched, to catch the tears before they got loose to slide down his cheeks and give him away. Guilt brought a pain within and he wasn't sure how to handle it. He hoped it would go away.

Perhaps he could change the subject. "Eny one fer a song? First good meal in a while an' it ain't too bad a night."

"Good idea," Foley agreed. "I'll git Cameron ta bring his harmonica. Let's git cleaned up 'n put some wood on the fire."

The dishes and utensils were cleaned and put up and the evening was spent in song. Sergeant Raymond, Willis, and several others joined the group to add their voices, too. The day's events were retold and news was shared by others as well. Lieutenant Jenkins brought word of the captain's decision to distribute the new clothing supplies following morning muster, and orders for company drill during the next day.

Darkness crept over the countryside. Candle lanterns were lit. The encampment winked with its thousand scattered fireflies. Tattoo called the troops to their tents, and taps settled them in their blankets.

*   *   *

Winter passed into Spring. As the weather warmed, the drill schedule increased. Companies drilled in the morning. Regiments drilled some afternoons and gathered for evening muster and review. Mr. Hasslett was as good as his word and delivered a wagon load of food supplies, a few used shoes, and an assortment of clothing. Beauty continued to mend as she thrived under the loving attention of Annie and the other youngsters of the family. It was as though she sensed she had to stay off her leg and was content to lie around as the center of attention.

Duane asked if he might visit later to see Beauty when she was back on her feet. What he really wanted was to get away from army life. There was a feeling of family warmth which lingered in his memory from the day he'd been there to help save the dog. He liked Annie. He liked a strange inner warmth that had been touched by the joy she had shown when he helped her Beauty. Mr. Hasslett got the captain's permission to have the boys out when the time came.

Tod had a new-found respect for his tentmate. He had someone to talk to who could understand his inner aching for his brother. He talked of Jason, remembering the things they'd done together and opinions shared and lessons learned. For the first time since he'd left home, Duane spoke of his mother in great detail, her likes and dislikes, reprimands for his foolishness such as the time he fed the livestock in mid-morning because they looked hungry, moments of warmth like the day the storm flooded the dam he and Jamie had built. The two boys developed a closer friendship and were frequently seen together in their travels about the camps. One day as the two paused to watch one of the Virginia artillery batteries at drill, they were surprised to observe a spunky youngster about Duane's age on one of the gun crews. When drill was finished, they stayed on to visit and to learn all about artillery warfare from a proud expert.

Near mid-March, word came of a great fight of cavalry at Kelly's Ford, nearly twenty-five miles northwest of Fredericksburg. The Federal cavalry force was unexpectedly well organized and proficient. It cost the Confederates dearly as they lost twice as many to casualties as did the Federals. A noted officer from Alabama, Major John Pelham, was killed in the engagement. He was well known to the men of Company K and much respected by his fellow officers right up to General Lee himself.

Early April brought an invitation to the Hasslett estate. Beauty had recovered enough to begin exercising her leg. Annie rode into the camp with her father to pick up Duane and Tod. She sure looked pretty, the younger boy thought. Both boys had bathed in the wooden washtub the night before. They wore their best clothes for the day's visit.

The beautifully mild day passed quickly as Duane and Tod roamed the farm property, enjoyed a picnic lunch with the other children, played with Beauty, and visited with the Hasslett family. Annie was the perfect hostess—polite and formal femininity as required, and the playful tomboy when permitted. All too soon, the boys were once again riding the wagon. As they returned to camp, chattering along the way, Duane suddenly realized there was little chance they'd get away from the camp again. It had been such a perfect day. He stared at Annie as she answered some question his friend had asked. She sure was beautiful.

He'd really miss her. He wished he could hold her. What were these strange feelings? He must be falling in love.

Annie caught him staring. She never broke her train of conversation, but she smiled. Duane felt himself blush and his face get hot.

Suddenly they were stopping. The wagon had reached the camp. A short time later it was gone again and Duane was standing alone, waving, and watching it disappear into the distance. Tod had already gone to build the fire for cooking supper.

*   *   *

In mid-April, the rains came. For over a week they continued to turn the countryside into a muddy quagmire. Finally, over the last weekend of the month, the skies cleared and brisk winds dried the mud. Within two days word came that Jeb Stuart's cavalry had reported Federal troops moving north along the river.

*   *   *

Wednesday's predawn light was just beginning to brighten the canvass when Willis burst frantically into the boys' tent.

"Hurry, Mass'rs!" he called. "Ya's gotta drum up the camp Mass'r Tod and the captain wants Mass'r Dee right quick. The Yanks is crossin the rive'."

"Damnation!" Tod exclaimed. "Sure a hell of a way ta be gittin a day goin!"

"Thet's fer sher!" Duane agreed. "Tell the captain as we's movin," he spoke to Willis.

The two boys dressed on the run as the drums began the long roll throughout the division. A hazy fog covered the riverlands, giving a ghostly cast to the camps. Tod took his position near the captain's tent and began his drum roll, the last of his clothes on the ground at his side. Duane suddenly realized he had left his gear behind out of everyday habit, and wasn't yet equipped for battle. Rushing back to the tent, he buckled on his gunbelt and grabbed the rest of his equipment, then hurried toward the captain's tent. Throughout the camp the men were stumbling forth in dazed and sleepy confusion.

"What's up, Tod?" Foley asked as he rushed up, still tucking in his shirt tail.

"Yanks comin," his nephew replied.

"But I ain't even brought ma gun!" Kim exclaimed as he overheard the conversation.

"Dee," Captain Rogers called from within his tent. "See Willis fer a mount, then git ta Colonel Fry's courier staff."

"Yes, Sir!" the boy acknowledged.

"Folla me, Mass'r Dee." Willis instructed.

Meanwhile, Lieutenants Guthries and Jenkins instructed the company to prepare immediately for an expected attack. The sergeants quickly issued ammunition and checked to be sure each man had gun, cartridge box, and gear. Loud and orderly confusion reigned throughout the regiment as companies of men were brought under arms and officers scurried about to learn the state of affairs.

Duane secured a frisky young stallion, roan in color, and rode off to regimental headquarters only to be sent on to General A. P. Hill's division headquarters. There it was learned that Federal troops had crossed on pontoon bridges and were entrenching in line along the river road under cover of Union batteries on the river's north bank. One of Lee's divisions had already deployed along the railroad embankment near the Old Richmond Road and another was in motion to reinforce it. General Hill was to bring his division into line along the crest of the ridge to the right. Duane carried the news back to Colonel Fry, then back to Captain Rogers. The troops were rushed into position. Poised for the attack, the armies faced each other expectantly. Nothing happened.

For Duane, there was little time for boredom as he kept busy relaying information. Messages from scouting reports came in through General Lee's staff to be relayed by the couriers to the various division and regimental commanders. During the afternoon, word came from General Stuart that Union troops had moved in force to cross the Rappahanock northwest of

Fredericksburg and were gathering at Chancellorsville. That night, a division was sent west to protect the Confederate left.

Thursday dawned with the Union army still entrenched at their river crossing. More reports came of Federal troops to the west. Finally, orders were given to leave one division facing the inactive Union bridgehead and march the rest of General Jackson's corps westward at dawn the following morning.

The day was spent packing field packs in preparation for the move. During a brief moment after delivering a message to Captain Rogers, Duane gathered his personal gear to be grabbed at the last minute. That night, all was in readiness for midnight muster.

As midnight passed in brilliant moonlight, the company struck camp and the corps prepared to move out. General Early's division remained in place along the railroad while the rest of the corps departed by the Old Mine Road, out of sight of the unsuspecting Federal force. When night slipped to a dense misty dawn the first day of May, Fredericksburg had been left miles behind as Jackson's troops advanced to join up with the divisions sent ahead the previous day.

For a while, Duane rode with General Hill's courier staff. He learned that two divisions were already engaging the enemy at the Tabernacle Church, about four miles east of Chancellorsville. Jackson was advancing to join them with four more divisions and more than a hundred and fifty pieces of field artillery. The boy sensed a growing excitement as he moved ever closer to certain battle.

An hour before noon, the elements of the Confederate Army came together. Brisk skirmishing began as Generals Lee and Jackson ordered their troops to advance and pressure the Yanks. Musket fire rattled along a two-mile front, mixed with Rebel yells. By nightfall, the Union pickets and skirmishers were forced back to their army encampments.

The boy was exhausted. He had been on the road relaying dispatches since before dawn. Duane spent the night in a forest glade beside the road. The division slept under arms, their heads pillowed on their packs. The officers conferred as plans were made to circle around and strike the Federal forces from behind their right flank. By dawn of the next morning, the troops were on the move. Silently they proceeded as the air echoed with the rhythmic clicking of bouncing canteens.

The ten-mile march took most of the day. For fifty minutes of every hour, the column advanced. After a ten-minute rest, it marched another fifty minutes. Duane heard gunfire to the rear of the column during the late morning and learned of a Federal attack which had been checked by remaining troops under General Lee. Word came around mid-afternoon that the troops of the Federal right were unaware of the Confederate move as they relaxed in the sun or slaughtered local beef cattle. Their weapons were all stacked. General Jackson also learned that the enemy lines extended beyond the road he had intended to use to outflank them. Thus it was late in the afternoon before his corps was in position to attack.

General Hill's division was third in line of march. The two front divisions had cleared the last dirt lane onto the turnpike to the west of the Federal defenses. Duane found himself with others of the courier staff crowded off the dirt roadway to allow the troops to pass. They slipped into a break between brigades and rode out to the turnpike where there was room to get off onto an open field.

A short distance up the roadway, General Jackson sat astride his little sorrel. With his watch in hand, he supervised the disposition of the troops as they arrived on the field. As quiet as 26,000 men can move, the brigades advanced from the wooded lane onto the turnpike and into position.

Duane saw that beyond the general, the front division was spread across the roadway to disappear almost a mile to either side. Thick woodland lay between the armies, preventing the enemy from viewing the massing for the attack. The boy watched as General Hill's division moved slowly into place. There was no sign of his regiment since it was advancing far off to the right of the turnpike. Glancing toward the sun, far to the west, yet still well up in the warm afternoon sky, he judged it to be between five and six o'clock. All was in readiness.

The front line began to advance into the thick woodland. Suddenly the woods echoed with the crackle of musketry as Union picket lines opened fire on the leading regiments. Immediately, Confederate buglers carried the call to charge and were joined all along the line by the blood-curdling Rebel yell. Ten thousand human voices shattered the evening quiet with such a fearful commotion as to stir up every living forest creature and drive it before the advancing onslaught. Rabbit, fox, and deer rushed in terror before the Confederate charge to race across the Union defenses and through the camps, busy with preparations for the evening meal.

Jackson and his generals followed in the thick of movement along the pike. Staff officers and courier riders kept nearby. The artillery was divided. Much was parked in a field on the right while some batteries advanced in column along the road.

Captain James Power Smith, assistant Adjutant-General, was the designated center of communication. Riding a black charger, he gathered his staff of couriers to maintain the flow of information from the point at which the charge had begun.

Ahead, the roar of artillery joined the thunderclaps of the leading ranks of rifle fire ripping into the first companies of Federal infantry. A few volleys of murderous musket fire seemed to check the advance briefly. Then the advance was swift and quickly outdistanced Duane and his comrades as the Union Army collapsed and fell back. Before the half hour was out, the sound of orderly gunfire had disintegrated into scattered pockets of fighting as the heavy underbrush and woodlands tore at the bodies of the men rushing through them, and fragmented regimental and company organization.

Duane listened to the distant sound of battle and thought of his friends in Company K. He wondered where they might be and was lost in thoughts for their welfare while all about him, officers and messengers came and went. His ponderings were rudely interrupted by one of Smith's aides.

"Private!" a young lieutenant called, "ride ahead to the farm house about a quarter mile on the right and see if General Hill is there. Tell him that artillery will be following."

"Yes, Sir," the boy responded as he dug his heels into his stallion's flanks and leaped into a run.

On the way, Duane crossed the first lines of battle where a fierce slaughter had taken place. Several hundred dead and wounded lay along the breastworks of earthen defenses that stretched across the road. A number of their comrades were attempting to help the wounded until ambulance wagons could arrive and carry them to the hospitals. At the farm house the battle was quickly advancing eastward as artillery was letting fly a terrible storm of shot and shell and the infantry continued to fire and advance on the enemy. Union troops were in a general route as they fled in panic before the deadly storm. The quick lightning of hundreds of rifles dealt death and damage from a dozen different directions.

Duane located one of the brigadier generals. "I've a message for General Hill," he hollered above the storm.

"He's moving toward the tavern yonder!" the general pointed.

The boy gazed at the panorama of war as far as the eye could see. Ten thousand men surged eastward as the Confederate brigades poured forth a murderous fire in a thousand flashes of riflery, and a wave of blue fell and ebbed in retreat or rallied briefly around some point to pause and fire back. Duane started forward to find the general when suddenly a line of Federal resistance took form at right angle to the road near the tavern. Artillery and rifle fire began to erupt in deadly explosions of canister and gunfire. Yet as each eruption mowed the road clear of advancing Confederates, a new wave replaced the one cut down.

Unexpectedly, Duane found himself in the midst of the violent fury with bullets picking at his clothing and shell fragments tearing at men as they screamed and fell nearby. Quickly he reined his horse to follow in the midst of regiments charging down a country lane to the right. Within minutes the mass of Rebel regiments was struck head on by a charge of Union cavalry. The roar of battle was deafening as a volley of Confederate rifle fire slammed into the advancing cavalry and stopped it dead in its tracks. In seconds more than two dozen cavalrymen and three times as many horses, lay dead or dying or wounded.

Muskets clattered and rifles shattered the countryside with violent death and destruction. Screams of men and animals rent the air as cannon shells crashed into massed humanity. Confusion and horror reigned as riderless horses panicked and cavalrymen on foot ran to catch a mount or seek cover. Men and animals ran into each other in their fearful dash for safety. Confederate infantry fired in volley at fleeing Union cavalry troopers caught afoot. Pack mules from the cavalry ran wild, tied in pairs and carrying their burdens of extra ammunition. Cannon shells exploded in the trees as rifle fire ripped along the ground. A panicked pair of mules being chased by a cavalryman in search of a mount, became tangled in a tree. A shell exploded in the tree, setting off the packs of ammunition and disintegrating the animals. As the murderous fire from the grey-clad soldiers cut down great numbers of men in blue, those who could, fled as fast as beast or foot would carry them. Weapons and packs were cast aside in their haste to get away.

Duane was unable to move. Caught in the pack of humanity, he was forced to the side of the road. Eventually the boy managed to move into a thicket, dense enough to force the tide of advancing Confederates to split and flow around it.

As the battle surged ever eastward, Union artillery was gathered on high ground about a mile from the tavern. Soon it sent forth a shower of death which slowed the Confederate front and gave the shattered Federals a chance to rally and establish a new line of defense.

71

Duane retreated, unable to find the general and deliver his message. Too much had happened and it seemed too late to make a difference. The Federals were quickly organizing a line of defense and more artillery was being brought to bear. The attack slowed as daylight faded and the boy worked his way back toward the main road.

Captain Smith was gathering together his staff and proceeding to join General Jackson when Duane came into view. All about the battle field, the Confederate units were trying to reorganize as they brought together the scattered companies and officers gathered their men.

"Hurry, Boy!" the captain called.

Duane rode to catch up

The couriers were gathered. The captain and his staff continued to seek the general. Twilight fell, and with it a silence. The party rode through groups of prisoners under guard, regiments trying to regroup, and wounded waiting under trees by the turnpike. Finally the captain's party approached an open field in which there were horsemen near a cabin.

Captain Smith recognized the officer in charge.

"General Rodes?" he called.

"General Jackson's ahead on the road, Captain," the general responded. "Tell him I will be here at this cabin if I am wanted."

"I'll do that," Smith replied.

As the group moved on, a pair of shots was heard. Then a company volley from the right was followed by a volley from the left. An officer whom Duane recognized from General Hill's staff, rode up in a panic.

"Generals Jackson and Hill are wounded and some with them are dead!" he called.

The group rushed forward at a gallop to lend assistance. They found Jackson in General Hill's arms, lying on the ground. Smith quickly dismounted to check the general's wounds. Cutting the senior officer's coat sleeve its full length, he took a handkerchief to tie off the flow of blood from a shattered arm. Duane and others were sent off in search of Doctor Hunter McGuire, corps surgeon and friend to the general, and for an ambulance. In the time it took to secure an ambulance, Captain Smith brought the general by litter within friendly lines, under a hazardous fire from the enemy. The boy returned with the ambulance and stayed with the staff as they left from the front.

"I must pull my men back and reorganize!" Brigadier-General Pender, commander of the troops in the immediate area, told the general.

"You must hold at all costs," General Jackson ordered his brigadier.

"What now?" an aide asked.

"Find Jeb Stuart," one of General Hill's aides instructed. "Pass the word we're moving forward."

As riders were sent out, the ambulance carrying the general proceeded to the tavern where a rest stop would be made.

"Private," Captain Smith turned to the boy, "I understand you're from General Archer's brigade of Hill's division."

"Thet's right, Sir."

"Earlier they were off to the right." The captain paused to check on the general. Continuing, he instructed, "We've pushed the line far enough that the road is open behind the lines."

"Which road?" Duane asked, worried about becoming lost in the dark of night.

"Hold a minute," the captain held his horse as the ambulance continued on. Turning to face a farm house they had just passed, he pointed out a road to the south. "See the road that cuts south behind the farm?" Duane nodded. "Follow it to where it forks, then keep south. The right of the line should be about a mile or two south from there."

"Thank ya, Sir," his voice quavered slightly from exhaustion and concern.

"The sky's night light and the broken moon'll see ya through. Go quickly and get some rest b'fore dawn. Tell General Archer ta go with first light."

"Yes, Sir. I'm on ma way."

The two parted and Duane pushed his stallion into an easy canter.

Traveling the country lane was easier than he had expected. It was alive with regiments from two of General Hill's brigades, as they shifted into position to renew the attack. Brigadier-General James Archer was with his brigade about a half mile from the fork in the road. Duane found him sitting by a tree with some of his staff. He rode up and dismounted.

"One a yer couriers, General," an aide observed.

"What news have you, Private?" the general asked.

"Generals Jackson and Hill was wounded, Sir, 'n General Stuart is in command," the boy reported.

"What!"

"Yes, Sir. Not mor'n fifty minutes back," Duane continued. "Captain Smith says fer me ta say fer the general as yer ta go with first light." Out of breath with exhaustion he added, "Will ya be needin me fer a bit?"

"No, Private. Where's yer company?"

"Company K of Colonel Fry's regiment, Sir."

"They're across the road in the woods behind the Virginia artillery. Get some sleep."

Duane walked in search of the company, leading his stallion by the reins.

The soldiers of the brigade lay in company formation in the woods and thickets straddling the road. Sleeping on the ground or against the trees, many rested with their weapons at their side or across their body. Captain Rogers and his lieutenants were standing near a small fire on which they'd brewed a pot of coffee. They looked up at the approaching shadows of horse and boy.

"Who's there?" the captain asked.

"Private Kinkade, Sir."

"Ya look like hell," Lieutenant Jenkins observed. "Ya okay?"

"Yes, Sir. Jest wore out 'n a bit messed from the fightin." He tied the horse to a tree.

"Here," Lieutenant Guthries offered a cup of lukewarm coffee.

"Thanks." The boy took the cup and drank slowly.

The men studied the boy while he drank. They had not yet been in the immediate conflict. He obviously had. His clothing was torn by bullets and fragments of shellfire, and his face and hands were blackened from gunsmoke and dirt, and streaked from sweat. Duane glanced along the lines of sleeping soldiers, searching for Tod and his drum. He found his tentmate about thirty yards off and was satisfied. Then he noticed some bandages among the men.

"Ya see much fightin?" the boy asked.

"Yeste'day it was a might fierce," Damien answered. "We was at the back end a the march 'n a Yank division hit behind. But General Lee brought up some brigades as were with him an took on the Yanks so as we could get along. There was others further back as got the worst of it."

"Ya git some sleep," Rogers ordered. "Tamorra ya take General Archer's report ta Hill."

"Hill ain't runnin thin's. He 'n Jackson was wounded."

"Hell, no!"

"Yes, Sir. General Heth has the division an Jeb Stuart's doin fer Jackson."

Duane described briefly the action he had seen and the wounding of the generals. Afterwards he settled by the tree to which his horse was tied. Resting his head on a rise in the root structure, he was soon fast asleep.

*　　*　　*

It was still dark when Willis shook Duane by the shoulder to awaken him.

"Here, Mass'r Dee," he offered. "Have a biscuit."

"Thank ya, Willis," he said. "What time is it?"

"Stars is fadin ta day," the youth answered.

All about them, the men were eating from the provisions they carried if they were hungry. The fire had been put out and the coffee pot packed. Duane untied his horse and stood by, ready to mount. Weapons were checked and the company was formed in line of battle. Orders were passed in whispers. The brigade was ready.

On the high ground in front, called Hazel Grove, the Federals had a strong position of artillery and infantry, capable of devastating the Confederate wing of Jackson's corps as well as the troops of General Lee's left about a mile to the east.

Confederate skirmishers were sent ahead to drive back the Federal pickets and to feel out the enemy's strength. As the light of dawn began to lighten the forest landscape, the sharp crackle of musketry opened to the front. Word came back that the Union force was withdrawing. Quickly the advance was ordered and the brigade charged the slope onto the hilltop. As the infantry moved forward, Colonel Alexander put his artillery batteries into motion. The guns, already hooked to their limbers, were rushed forth to be placed into position on the hill.

General Archer, easily spotted for his slight build and long beard, followed the movement closely. Duane mounted and rode over to join the general's staff and observe the action. Riding toward the fighting, they entered the smoke of battle and observed the excitement of success as the Confederate troops rounded up some hundred prisoners and added a handful of captured artillery pieces to the lineup.

Searching for signs of the Alabama 13th, Duane's attention was distracted by the artillery as he caught sight of the youngster he'd met previously, enthusiastically helping to prepare his gun. After several minutes, the batteries began to open against the Federal position to the east. The boy worked the lanyard to his gun. Duane smiled as he watched him pull the lanyard to fire the charge, roll about on the ground in clownish glee, then jump to his feet and grab the lanyard to fire again.

Meanwhile, General Archer wrote out a brief description of the action to be sent ahead to General Stuart.

"Private," he called to Duane, "take this pouch to Stuart and add any information ya learn along the way."

"Yes, Sir. On the way." He slung the bags across the saddle in front of him and started back toward the road.

Duane listened to the orderly thunder of the guns in Hazel Grove as he worked his way through the regiments which had not yet engaged. Once clear of the brigade and its support wagons, he leaned into a gallop to race north toward the turnpike.

The boy courier had just begun his race along the road when the guns to the north opened on the enemy. Shells shrieked through the air and the ground beneath him trembled as the cannon roared forth a hellish rain of death and destruction all along the line. Clouds of smoke rose through the trees. Within minutes, the charge was sounded and the infantry attacked with ferocious firepower.

Riding the road in the earliest light of day, Duane entered the reserve lines of General Rode's corps. There he was directed to the farm house on the turnpike where he was relieved of the courier pouch and sent forth to gather information on Brigadier-General McGowan's brigade, advancing on Archer's left.

McGowan's brigade was heavily engaged in the woods less then six hundred yards beyond the house and just south of the road. Duane rushed forward into an explosive hellfire of searing musketry and tree-splitting cannon shell. At the moment, the Confederates were advancing. Fierce fighting surrounded the young rider as he debated pushing further to find the general. Shells exploded in the trees overhead, splintering branches and sending large limbs smashing to the ground below. Shrapnel from exploding shell fragments ripped through the tree-tops and tore through the movement of advancing infantry. A new sound was evident in the smoke-filled forest—the crackle of fire. In several places, the woods and underbrush had burst into flame.

Suddenly a sheet of rifle fire roared into the ranks on the right, cutting down grey-clad soldiers in waves. The stallion rose up on its hind legs, screaming in pain as a swarm of bullets

77

ripped through the screaming, yelling mass of troops around the boy. He felt pain as a bullet burned across the back of his hand. A tree limb came crashing down on a company to the left, felling a dozen unsuspecting soldiers. Flames spread noisily in the underbrush, engulfing the wounded caught in its path. Union soldiers advancing on the right pushed the Confederates back. Wounded of both armies clung to trees, frantically pushing away the brush and leaves at their feet in hope of staying the flames. Still they came.

All about the boy on the screaming horse, the woods were full of cries, gunfire, and crackling flames. Trying to stay with the crazed stallion, Duane found himself on the verge of panic. Still on its hind legs, the horse staggered to the side. Duane heard the impact of a half dozen bullets ripping into his mount's chest and belly and cringed with the expectation of bullets striking his own body. Instead, he found himself falling as the stallion toppled backwards and pinned the boy under its corpse.

The brigade fell back in retreat, taking along whomever of the wounded that could be gathered up. Not far to the left another Confederate brigade was being swept back. Pinned beneath his dead horse, Duane struggled to free himself. Grabbing the saddle, he pulled himself up and saw the horror as several dozen dazed survivors milling about in confusion, were mowed down at point-blank range by advancing Federals. Screams of pain, the crashing roar of infantry fire, and the crackling conflagration of burning forest made a living, breathing, crying, fear-filled hell. The boy pushed frantically with his free foot in terrified attempts to break free. Inch by inch he drew himself from beneath the weight of the animal as movement of men in battle surged through the surrounding woodland.

New gunfire erupted behind the Confederate front. Fresh brigades were entering the battlefield, rushing through the ranks of the retreating. As the Union troops fired into the collapsing brigade, the new arrivals flung themselves on the ground and began firing over the heads of their retiring comrades. Duane hugged the ground close to the stallion's back, hoping to stay low enough to remain safe. Circulation in the pinned leg had been restricted by the pressure of weight and the boy felt a loss of feeling as the leg went numb.

Some of the retreating were wounded by their own rescuers. The rest dropped and froze in place. The advancing Confederates did the same. Their officers could do nothing to budge them as fear took command.

Caught in the middle, Duane looked to the front where Federal forces were massing for a counter attack. Two more Confederate brigades came to the rescue and poured a devastating fire into the Federal line, pushing it back. Shortly after they began to push forward, Union infantry returned such an exploding hail of lead as to decimate the leading edge of grey, mortally wounding both commanding generals.

Again the position was in danger of being overrun by men in blue. The rescuing Southern brigades fell back, exhausted. They included the Stonewall Brigade which had been involved in so much of the action because of its strength and experience. They were worn out. Yet once again they advanced, this time under the personal encouragement of General Stuart.

For Duane, time had been an eternity. Now the tide was turned and the Federals were driven back upon their own artillery, about a half mile back. A passing soldier helped Duane free himself from his horse, then moved on. The storm of battle continued to tear its way through the wooded wilderness. The fires burned in patches about the forest and underbrush. The boy dragged himself toward a broken tree. There he sat and rubbed his leg to regain circulation and feeling. Prickling needles of pain gave way to weakness. Eventually Duane was able to stand tentatively before hobbling aimlessly toward a company of survivors, debating their next course of action.

Deciding there was little left for him to do, Duane joined the efforts to help the wounded. He found himself unhurt, but bloodied from his horse's wounds and from the bloodied forest floor. The scene was one of horror. Dead and wounded carpeted the blood-soaked ground as far as one could see in all directions. Charred corpses hugged the trees where the fire had caught the wounded. Others littered the charred thickets where they had fallen and died. Cries and pleadings of the wounded added a mournful wail to the sound of battle strong in the distant fighting and artillery fire.

The battle ebbed by mid-morning as the Union Army pulled back and prepared to retreat. Duane busied himself throughout the morning in the efforts to save the wounded. He found it hard to believe that some he found were still alive. Ripping fabric from whatever was at hand, the boy worked quickly to stem the flow of bleeding and to keep the battlefield wounded alive for the surgeon's table. Working his way across the battlefield, he found his way to the edge of the tree line opening onto Hazel Grove. By noon he found his way back to his own company in his own brigade.

The guns were quiet on Hazel Grove. General Lee and his staff had gone ahead to the Chancellor House where the Union command had been. Many of the batteries of artillery from early morning had been moved farther to the front. The field was scattered with fragments of the brigade, still recovering or regrouping from the morning's fighting. Wounded were being attended and the dead were being gathered for burial. Company K was gathered with others of the regiment. Duane was overjoyed to find his companions. He approached at a very tired walk and noticed the men of the company had dropped in disorderly exhaustion wherever they had been when the fighting had stopped.

"Where's the captain, Sergeant?" the boy asked the first person he found.

"Where's yer horse?" Sergeant Matthewson asked upon recognizing the courier on foot.

"Shot out from under me," Duane explained.

"The captain's hurt bad, Dee. They took him off early this mornin," the sergeant answered. "Lieutenant Jenkins is in charge 'n he's talkin ta Willis an' Sergeant Raymond on supplies."

The man pointed to the trio in conversation near a supply wagon about twenty yards off.

Approaching the conference, Duane waited respectfully to be noticed.

"Our wanderin' boy has returned," the sergeant acknowledged.

"Dee," the lieutenant asked, "could ya see ta Tod? He ain't lookin' much good an ain't sayin' much neither."

"Yes, Sir," the boy replied. "How's Captain Rogers an' when d' I git duty?"

"Dunno 'bout the captain. Lots a officers is hurt an' the general's doin' fer General Heth an' the colonel's doin' fer the general. We stay put till orders is passed."

"Yes, Sir. I'll look ta Tod, now."

"Thanks, Dee. He's layin' yonder where's Kim an' Foley kin keep watch on him."

Duane found his friend very pale and only half conscious.

"What happened?" the younger boy asked.

"Don't rightly know," Foley answered from where he knelt beside his nephew. "He was near the end a the company by the captain when a enemy shell exploded in the air. Near 'bout a dozen went down from our company an' the next. Four was killed outright 'n Captain Rogers tore up bad. But Tod got up 'n looked okay."

"Thet you, Dee?" a feeble voice asked. "Ya look real bad hurt."

Duane dropped by the older boy's feet. "Yea, Tod, it's me. But I ain't hurt. What's wrong?"

"Ain't knowin' fer sher." He winced from sharp pain. "Is ma legs both there? I cain't feel two, but cain't say as what's missin'." He paused, tired from the effort to talk. "God, it hurts!" he whispered.

"Kim," Duane instructed the youth beside whom the drum lay, "I need Tod's drumsticks and strap."

"What fer?"

"Jest hurry." There was a panic in the voice that ended any question.

81

Duane slipped the strap under both legs and lay the sticks between.

"Hold his shoulders," the boy instructed as he grabbed a boot by its heel and toe. His eye caught sight of a flaw—a hole through the upper leather. Releasing his grip, he tied the strap around the leg, just above the boot top, and slipped a drumstick into the knot.

"What fer ya doin thet?" Kim asked.

"Jest hold him an ya'll see."

Once more he gripped the boot and eased it off.

"Oh, God!" Kim gasped. The boot spilled forth a puddle of blood as it revealed sock and pant leg saturated and dripping with blood.

Quickly Duane tightened his tourniquet.

"What happened?" Foley asked.

Duane held the boot so they could see the hole. "Seems a fragment a thet shell shot through 'n inta his leg. Lucky he ain't bled ta death. But still we could be too late. Kin ya find some bandages? Ya best fix ta git him ta the hospital, too."

As Kim went to see his brother for bandages and transportation, the boy sent Foley for a bottle or keg of whiskey. Corporal Robert DiPhilippo and Private Matthew Guthries, who were nearby, came to offer their help. Others became aware of what was happening and turned to watch. Sergeant Raymond joined them as soon as he learned from Kim that Tod's condition was discovered.

Duane found a knife and carefully cut open the bloody trouser leg, then peeled off the saturated sock.

"What fer ya'd do thet?" Tod asked faintly.

"Yer shot through the leg," his friend answered. "We gotta git ya fixed up."

Satisfied his friend knew what he was doing, the wounded boy relaxed and drifted into unconsciousness. Robert and Matthew helped expose the wound and offered their canteens to wash away the blood. Duane examined the wound along with the sergeant.

"Don't look broke," the man announced. "But thet piece a shell's still in there. Ain't no second hole."

Duane agreed. Foley returned with a half bottle of whiskey which the boy took and opened. Kim returned with some bandages while half the whiskey was being poured over the wound. The wound was wrapped and the fabric soaked with the rest of the brew.

"Keeps it from festerin bad," the boy explained in answer to the quizzical looks from those around.

A wagon arrived and Tod was sent on to the hospital.

"Ya best go with him, Foley," the sergeant instructed. "Be sure ta bring back thet drumstick an' strap. The new drummer boy'll need em."

"Who's thet?" Duane asked.

"You, of course," Sergeant Raymond replied. "Ya've done afer. Ya kin do it now. We need you, Boy," he cocked his head and cracked a smile. "Yer too valuable ta be off doin courier."

*   *   *

As Sunday ended and nightfall darkened the countryside, the armies rested quietly. Their soldiers were tired. Those on picket duty settled in quickly with no interest in harassing each other. General Archer's brigade, now under the command of Colonel Fry, had been moved forward to press the attack against the retreating Federals. But word come of a new threat from the Union forces back in Fredericksburg. The divisions at Chancellorsville settled in along the turnpike while General Lee turned his attention to the potential danger from behind. The troops slept where they lay, having taken their leisure to cook a supper of salt beef, beans, fried bread, and coffee.

Foley had returned to report that Tod was very critical. He had lost so much blood, and only time would tell if he could hang on to recover or take sick and die. The youth had brought back the bloodied strap and stick as the sergeant had instructed, and

Duane had collected together all that remained of his friend's gear to keep with his own.

Monday saw little change in the brigade's situation. It remained in its position across from the Union center. As the day passed, another division was sent toward Fredericksburg to check the new Federal offensive. At Chancellorsville, the divisions remained poised but inactive. Tod's relations took advantage of the calm and went to visit him. Duane sent his tentmate's gear along, knowing he would probably be sent on to a proper hospital as he got stronger.

Throughout the day a fierce battle was fought miles away, while quiet reigned along the turnpike. By evening it was evident that Tod was hanging on. Word came, too, that Captain Rogers had lost an arm, but was expected to recover.

The night was spent in the open as soldiers slept in line of battle. Tuesday brought word that the distant fighting had ended when the enemy retreated across the river. Rain came early in the day and soaked the countryside all day long. Some companies set tentlines alongside the roadway. Many just stood around in wet misery with an oilcloth raincoat draped across their shoulders, if they owned one. Duane sat on the drum which he had turned on its side, and draped the great blue overcoat across his shoulders. His brimmed hat offered some protection at first. But eventually everything was saturated with rainwater and there was nothing to do but sit amongst the thousands and wait in misery for the storm to pass.

As another day dawned, the weather cleared and it was learned that the whole Union Army had pulled back across the river and was retreating to its camps at Fredericksburg. The Confederate Army did the same. Three days later, Duane found himself and his comrades back in the camp they'd left the previous week.

*　*　*

May passed into June. At mid-month General Lee had gone to meet with President Davis in Richmond to discuss his plans for the next campaign. After his return, he had reorganized the army into three corps. General Jackson had died of his wounds on Sunday the tenth and was sorely missed as new leadership was selected. General Longstreet's command continued in the I Corps. Jackson's II Corps would be commanded by Lieutenant-General Richard S. Ewell. General Archer's brigade became part of the new III Corps under the command of Lieutenant-General Ambrose Powell Hill.

The passing weeks had been spent in a routine of drill and foraging. There had been visits to the hospital in Fredericksburg to which the wounded from Chancellorsville had been brought. Some who hadn't seemed so badly wounded had died from blood poison. Others went through a rough time of pain and infection before healing. Captain Rogers was among them. Tod was one of the lucky ones who began their recovery early and continued to do well.

The first day of June saw great excitement as the soldiers shared their opinions on the new organization and leadership which had been announced the day before. There was also an air of high expectation and enthusiasm as the general's plans to invade the north became the talk of the newspapers and the driving energy for the soldiers.

A warm sun played peek-a-boo with white banks of clouds as Willis and Duane plodded along the River Road on their way back to camp. Fishing had been profitable, and each carried a string of bass and some trout in one hand and a fishing line rolled on a stick of wood in the other.

"Sher were a good ketch, Mass'r Dee," Willis commented. "Supper'll be a good change from salt pork as is gittin strong."

"Ya mean rottin spoilt-like," the boy added. "It does smell some when it cooks an' could twist yer innards good 'cept fer some sugar ta help the taste."

The air was vibrant with the movement of wagons and equipment and the activity of men and companies busy at drill, foraging, camp chores; or relaxed about their camps. The smell of the army blended with its sights and sounds to invade the senses with the aromas of latrines, animals, fire smoke, and unclean bodies. Across the river, the Union Army kept active in its camps.

The boy and his black companion paused to watch a couple of rowdy young infantrymen stir up a whirl of dust as each attempted to wrestle the other to the ground. Scores of cheering comrades encouraged the combatants as they wagered everything from cash money to coffee to boots on the outcome of the fray.

"Who ya think's gonna win?" Duane asked.

"Whatcha say fer the big guy?" Willis offered.

"May be," the boy responded, unconvinced.

"Not too sure?"

"No."

"Ya seein somethin in the other soldier?"

"He does 'pear ta be fast," Duane smiled.

"Sher does." A grin of agreement revealed Willis's teeth.

They waited a few more minutes, watching expectantly for the match to end. Suddenly, the smaller man saw an opening, dove for his opponent's knees, and drove him backwards to the ground.

The air erupted with wild cheers and yells as Duane and Willis turned to continue on their way. The sound of an approaching horse caused them to look ahead. A grey horse with black mane and tail walked toward them bearing a regal rider.

"Aftanoon, Mass'r Robert," the boy greeted. "How's Traveler taday?"

"He's just fine, Soldier," the general replied, easing his horse to a stop. "Mighty fine string of fish you have there. Your company will be mighty pleased to see you."

"Thank ya, Sir," Duane returned. "When da we git ta movin north? Here tell we's gittin ta some good foragin in Maryland and Pennsylvania."

"All in good time, Son," Lee replied. "You see your friends eat well and are ready when the time comes."

"Yes, Sir, Mass'r Robert."

The two waved as they continued on their way and the general acknowledged before he rode on.

Arriving in camp, the youth and the boy went about giving away their fish to those present who wished to clean and cook them. Keeping a couple each, Willis returned to headquarters and Duane looked up Kim and Foley. Along the way, he passed Corporals Robert DiPhilippo and Howard Griffin.

"Too bad yer not the company's drummer no more," Robert teased as he set a sock of coffee grounds into the pot of water.

"Yeh," Howard added while adding kindling to the newly lit cook fire. "We was jest gittin use ta ya."

Duane stopped, hurt by the news. "Why fer? Ain't I doin good by ya all?"

"Sher ya are," Howard agreed.

"But we come by this real neat feller as we's wantin real bad inta the company." Robert paused as he set the coffee pot onto the fire. "Ya has ta see Kim and Foley. Theys'll set ya straight an gives ya sompin else ta do."

The two men smiled as if all was a joke. A disheartened boy wandered to the cousins' tent.

Kim and Foley were seated in front of their tent, busy preparing beans and coffee for dinner.

"Brought us some fish," Duane offered as he approached.

"Thanks," Foley reached for the offering. "Ya gonna he'p clean em?"

"Sher." Duane drew out a knife and settled beside the fire where he found a tin plate on which to work.

"Why so gloomy?" Kim asked.

"Robert an' Howard said as I wasn't needed no more fer ta do the drummin."

"They say why?"

"Jest as ya's got some real neat fella as is wanted in the company."

"Thet sure was mighty nice a them ta care so," a third voice joined from behind.

Duane turned as he recognized it. "Tod! Sher as tarnation is!" He jumped to his feet.

The two stood staring at each other.

"Go ahead," Foley encouraged. "Ya kin hug each other. Yer same as family an' we's already done ar share."

The two embraced in the joy of finding themselves together once more.

"Doc says as ya saved ma life," Tod said, somewhat subdued with emotion.

"Oh, God, I'm so glad yer okay 'n back. Thet tent sher is mighty lonely." The younger boy stepped back to study his friend. "Damn, you look good."

"Yer a fine sight, too," Todd declared. "But I do detect the definite smell a fish. What ya say I lend a hand an' we fix em up fer fryin."

"Good idea."

The four settled to fixing dinner. Throughout the camp, others of the company were doing the same and the air about took on a fine aroma of fish frying in several iron skillets.

As evening settled, several arrived to share the news gathered from the day's travels and to learn what news Tod might have gathered in the hospital. The drummer boy had heard of plans to advance north and shared a number of combat stories he had heard. The captain, he added, was healing slowly and had been sent to Richmond for a time. He would return by end of summer. Some who had been foraging had found little or done some hunting instead. All shared that the common talk was of the planned invasion. Duane and Willis told of their passing General Lee on the River Road and his confirmation of the intended movement.

The talk passed. A harmonica and a fiddle were brought out by Cameron Doherty and a friend from the other platoon, and the group turned its attention to song. **DIXIE** led off, followed by **BONNIE BLUE FLAG**, and a number of other favorites. Lively songs gave way to love ballads, then the sadder songs of lost friends, mother, and home. Candle lamps were lit as the last light settled in the west and sparkling blackness reached up out of the east. Throughout the camps the smell of smoke and the smell of coffee blended with the sounds of insects and of the frogs along the river to mix with the quiet murmur of ten thousand quiet conversations. The countryside flickered with the firelight of a myriad tiny lanterns and the June bugs. Across the river another army shared the same routine.

*　　*　　*

The move north began midweek. Two divisions of the I Corps were sent to a meeting place called Culpeper. The II Corps followed the next day. General Hill was to hold his III Corps in its camps on a regular routine to keep the enemy occupied. The order was passed to send personal trunks to the rear and to pack light for the operation to come. Those in Company K who had anything to ship, sent those items to be held in Richmond, care of Captain Rogers. He was convalescing with relatives there and would take care of anything his men sent.

Over the next week and a half, the III Corps did as it was instructed and the Union Army remained in place across the river. Meanwhile, news came of a heavy cavalry engagement in the early part of the week and of combat at Winchester in the Shenandoah Valley.

On Monday of the following week, the III Corps followed the same route as the II Corps before it. By midweek it was at Culpeper. There the men were instructed to cook three days rations and pack them in their haversacks. Rations for another three days were carried in the regimental wagon. Still more were carried in the corps' supply train.

The end of the week found the corps at Chester Gap crossing the Blue Ridge Mountains into the valley of the Shenandoah. From there it was north toward the Potomac River at Shepherdstown. By this time, advance divisions from General Longstreet's corps were already in Pennsylvania.

The second week of the march began. Company K was in the midst of the long stretch of advancing infantrymen. The road was crowded as the officers pushed their men to keep the ranks closed. The day was hot as the soldiers bumped elbows and tripped over each others' feet in order to maintain the pace. A great whirling cloud of dust rose up along the miles of moving troops, choking the men and burning their eyes. The lush beauty of the Shenandoah farmland was lost to the men as they concentrated on moving ever forward. It was just as well; there was nothing left of its bounty. The Shenandoah had already been stripped as earlier campaigns saw first one army and then the other living off the land. At night, the troops bivouacked where they stopped, sleeping in the fields or woodlands alongside the road, only to rise the next morning to continue their march.

Word was passed down through the divisions to the regiments and their companies that General Lee had issued general order number 72 which gave strict instructions to officers and their men as to how they could procure supplies and carry out foraging expeditions while in the enemy's countryside, towns, and cities. All must be acquired in a civil manner. Nothing was to be taken or destroyed. No one was to be hurt. The Confederate soldier did not war on women and children.

Duane and his companions crossed into Union territory on Wednesday as the corps crossed the Potomac River at Shepherdstown and entered the state of Maryland. On the following day, they entered Pennsylvania to pass north through Greencastle and to follow General Ewell's corps through Chambersburg. There Hill headed east to end the week in camp at Fayetteville, where the divisions set their camps during the day. Fires were lit to cook dinner and companies put up their tents for the night.

A footweary bunch of filthy and ragged soldiers settled to a cooked meal from the spoils collected on the passage through town. The men of Company K reflected on the day's events over dinner. The local militia had fled at the sight of the advancing army. Just as well, Tod had observed, as someone could have been hurt. The local citizens had lined the streets in a quiet sullen humor to watch the army pass. Confederate soldiers had been placed to guard the homes of wealthy and prominent citizens according to general order 72, to prevent looting by members of the army. The town had been ordered to turn over specified goods and produce, some of which it had; thus allowing for the soldiers to live off the land without destroying property or harming the citizenry.

One soldier had been overheard to address a small crowd of frightened women, "You have nothing to fear from this dust-covered army of ragged-looking soldiers. We are at heart Christian and knightly men and protectors of children and womanhood."

Sunday dawned with first muster after daybreak. Breakfast was cooked, then the camps were struck in preparation for whatever orders might come. Once preparations for the march had been completed, the brigades rested along the roadside in line of march, or gathered in a field with their chaplain for Sunday services.

Tod sat with his drum at his side. Duane returned from helping Willis pack provisions in a wagon for the company. The wagon had gone off to join the division's supply train and the boy had joined his friend for the march.

"What ya think a company quartermaster type duty?" Tod asked.

"It's toler'ble," Duane replied. "Bein 'round the officer talk ya git ta hear what's happenin'."

"Eny news?" Tod drummed his sticks on the side of his drum in boredom.

"General Early sent word thar's a shoe fact'ry ahead in Gettysburg. Thet's a town 'bout twenty miles from here. General Ewell's marchin on the capital at Harrisburg. So far, there's no word on the Yank army, an' all the towns 'long the way is surrenderin."

"Sounds easy," Matthew Guthries added from nearby. He was carrying the company banner for the march.

"Jest so's they keep feedin us well," Tod said.

"I could git use ta this kind a northern hospitality," Sergeant Raymond stated as he approached. "Jest now, we's got orders. So on yer feet."

"Whar to?" Guthries asked.

"Ta jine the march on Harrisburg," the sergeant replied.

But the march did not begin. It was past noon before the corps was ready to move. They moved east along the pike. Cashtown lay about ten miles down the road. From there they would turn north to join General Ewell's corps and attack the capital. That night the corps bivouacked around Cashtown. During the early hours after midnight, new orders came. The Confederate Army was to gather at Cashtown. The Yanks were on the move. General Hill was to stay where he was and wait.

The III Corps was spread out along the pike. General Heth's Division was in the front. Elements of the I Corps were also in the line of march. As the army corps began to gather, the lead divisions settled along the pike, just east of Cashtown, about ten miles from Gettysburg. They were settled in and waiting by the last day of the month, with little to do but rest until the remaining divisions were gathered.

A quiet morning drifted lazily beyond breakfast. Men occupied their time in cards or gambling, or gazing at the rich farmlands that stretched to the gentle hills and distant ridges. Many of the platoon's dozen lay along the berm of the road—their muskets stacked, their eyes closed, their minds dreaming of home. The crunch of moving troops brought them quickly to their senses as a brigade headed on down the packed surface of the pike.

"Where they headed to, Lieutenant?" Cameron asked as he sat up and observed the company's officers standing nearby.

"Rememb'r thet shoe factory we heard 'bout?" Lieutenant Jenkins answered as he watched the units disappearing down the road.

"Yes, Sir."

"They's bin sent on ta git us a supply a shoes while we sits and waits on the rest a the army."

The wait continued. Duane and Tod spent the midday in small talk and their own projections as to what events lay ahead. By mid-afternoon, Brigadier General Pettigrew returned from Gettysburg with most of his brigade and staff. Some had remained on the road ahead on picket duty.

"Somethin musta happened," Tod observed. "Wonder where the brigade is?"

"Dunno," Duane responded. "Think I'll wander over ta see if Lieutenant Jenkins needs a runner."

The boy reported to the lieutenant to see if he were needed for courier staff and was sent on to Colonel Fry who sent him on to division headquarters. Several on courier detail milled around division staff as they waited for further instructions. They remained quiet in order to overhear the conversation between General Heth and General Pettigrew. Lieutenant-General A. P. Hill rode up in the midst of the discussion.

"As I stood on the ridge and surveyed the town through my field glasses, I observed a large column of Federal cavalry approaching fast on the road from Emmitsburg," Pettigrew reported. "In as much as we were after shoes and not a fight, I've withdrawn along the Chambersburg Pike to a point four miles from the town."

"That's very unlikely," Hill put in. "The enemy are still at Middleburg and have not yet struck their tents."

"Then if there is no objection, General, I will take my division tomorrow and get those shoes," Heth offered.

"None in the world," Hill replied.

Duane carried the report back that the division was preparing to move out and would advance to join Pettigrew's pickets. From there they would move on Gettysburg at dawn in order to get those shoes. The enemy, however, was present, and a fight was expected.

As night fell, a feeling of apprehension grew in the boy's stomach. He lay alongside his older friend in the edge of a meadow, his head pillowed on his pack, gazing at an overcast sky.

"Looks like rain," Tod stated.

"Kinda does," Duane agreed. "Ya skart?" he glanced toward his friend.

"Yeh," Tod answered. "I git real tight hurtin inside 'fer every battle when I knows as there's gonna be one."

"Tod," Duane whispered, "I fears it'll be bad tamorra. If I go down, could ya send a letter ta my home town and say as where I'm buried? Could be my pa'll git home an' wanta know."

"Ya ain't gonna die, Dee," Tod whispered back. "Enyway, I'll do fer you if'n ya's promise the same fer me."

"It's a promise." The two reached instinctively for each other's hand and shook on it.

They lay there for a while longer listening to the quiet breeze of a thousand soldiers sighing in the night as their thoughts dwelt on tomorrow. The insects were loud in their night songs. Cattle lowed softly in distant pastures. Dogs barked in distant farm yards. The night deepened and the army slept.

* * *

Tod, Duane, and many in the company awoke in the dark hours before dawn to the discomfort of an early morning drizzle. The whole division was roused before five as preparations began for the march on Gettysburg. A cold breakfast was taken from the provisions in the haversack which Willis had passed out the previous evening.

"Hurry up," Lieutenant Guthries whispered. "Git in line with yer platoon. We's pullin' out eny minute now."

"Mass'r Dee," Willis approached with some cumbersome collection in his arms. "Mass'r Jenkins said as you's ta have this musket 'n gear. Even if ya does git ta run messenger some, he wants ya ready ta fight if needs be."

"Thank ya, Willis." The boy accepted the equipment. "I'll do what needs doin'."

The black youth helped the boy with his belt and cartridge pouch, then left for other duties.

"It'll be good ta know yer nearby," Tod said, strapping on his drum and tightening the heads.

"Let's move out," a voice in the dark commanded.

By five in the morning, General Heth had his division on the road. Advancing ghostlike in the drizzly dawn, the column moved without comment along the pike. The sound of shoes in unison, crunching on the hard-packed surface, and of canteens clicking against cartridge belts, blended softly with the rainfall. It was nearly 5:30 as the first brigade approached a stone bridge across a small creek, nearly hidden by bottomland mists hanging over the water. A regiment of General Pettigrew's brigade had spent the night on picket, encamped on the west side of the bridge. As the column approached, they gathered in order, prepared to join their brigade. General Archer, riding at the head of the column, guided his horse to the side of the road to let his brigade pass.

Suddenly, a single rifle shot rang out; then silence.

"Skirmishers to the front!" The word was whispered down the ranks.

The skirmishers from Archer's brigade moved quickly to cross the bridge and spread out to the right of the road. The brigade followed to take the right of the road in line for battle. General Davis's brigade followed onto the left of the road. In the distant mist, the sounds of retreating horsemen could be heard falling back to a ridge just ahead. Cautiously the Confederates advanced. There was a burst of musketry as the Union cavalrymen engaged the line of skirmishers then fell back. A squadron of Federal cavalry continued a slow retreat, keeping up a continuous rifle fire. The cavalrymen dismounted and engaged the advancing brigade for a few minutes, then mounted to fall back and repeat the deployment.

After two miles of slow skirmishing and forward march, the infantrymen felt the terrain rise in front as it lifted across a ridge. The two leading brigades of the division paused on the crest near a building on the left of the pike identified as Herr's Tavern. As eight o'clock neared, the drizzle and rising mists had given way to a clear sun, and the panorama of fields, farms, woodlots, and gentle rolling ridges could be seen clearly in the quiet countryside surrounding the distant town of Gettysburg.

A thin line of Federal horsemen was evident in the lowland along a creek that crossed at the bottom of the ridge. At their right and straddling the road, was a battery of horse artillery. Beyond was another ridge with a farm where the road crossed its crest, flanked by fields with woodlot rising from the stream at the middle of the valley toward the crest of the ridge. The brigades advanced to the attack.

General Davis's brigade moved forward along the left of the road. General Archer led his troops past the crest of the ridge on the right, across from the farm and its woodlands. The regiments, formed in line of battle, stretched about a half mile along the top of the ridge. Nearly a thousand men made up the five regiments of Alabama and Tennessee infantrymen, with the 13th Alabama just right of center. The division's batteries of field artillery were strategically located across the pike at the height of the ridge.

Regimental flags and company banners hung on the morning air as the Federal line kept up a continuous fire. The soldiers stood poised with weapons loaded. Tod held his sticks over the drum head. Duane waited at his side. The order was passed along the lines.

"Advance," the lieutenant stated.

Tod struck the cadence as other company drummers did the same. The line of grey and butternut brown began to flow down the slope of the ridge toward the stream below with regimental flags to the front and companies dressed smartly on the colors. The morning sun glinted off the ranks of gun metal as orders rang out and muskets were brought to ready.

Advancing first, the skirmishers continued to draw fire all along the stream's course.

"Fire!"

"Fire!"

The order carried along the slope as the regiments fired in ranks, sending a deadly volley of lead into the underbrush below. Union cavalrymen returned the fire in rapid succession, faster than the attacking Rebels could reload.

"What the hell they usin'!" Sergeant Henson exclaimed.

"Here tell there's a new repeatin' rifle!" Lieutenant Guthries called above the noise of battle. "Stay low! And keep firing!"

The soldiers reloaded and fired at will while moving across open pastureland, then a small wheat field, in route to the thickets along the stream. Using whatever cover they could find to keep from getting hit, the advancing regiments pressed the Union line to give ground. Bullets rang against rocks, splintered branches and vegetation, kicked up the dirt, and whined through the air. All along the valley, a cloud of gunsmoke began to gather in the air as the smell of burnt powder grew pungent. There were the cries from the wounded and the shouts of orders. The Union battery of artillery opened fire and shells screamed through the air and exploded along the sloping ground. For nearly an hour, the fighting was a standoff. Then, gradually, the Union forces began to pull back up the western face of their ridge, giving as little ground as possible. The brigade advanced to a fence line parallel to the stream, then to the thickets along the stream. So far, casualties were light.

"Keep it up, lads!" Colonel Fry encouraged. "We're wearin' 'em down."

The battle wore on as the brigade continued its slow advance. Word was passed to prepare for a charge. It was only Union cavalry in front. General Pettigrew had said that yesterday and, so far, that's what had been seen. Moreover, they were withdrawing.

At mid-morning the order was given to charge. The bugles sounded, the drums rolled, the men yelled their wild challenge which struck fear into the hearts of their enemies. The thousand surged forward, across the run and up the slopes of the facing ridge.

A sudden volley ripped into the right flank from the acres of woodland behind the the farm and in the center of the face of the ridge.

"They ain't cavalry!" someone shouted as they caught sight of the adversary. "It's them damned black-hatted fellows!"

"It ain't militia!" another shouted. "It's the Army of the Potomac!"

The regiment at the right fell back and soon the Union troops broke from the woods and began to flank the brigade and move across its back. Fighting became fierce as Archer's troops turned to retreat. As the right pushed into the center of the line and more companies broke and ran, the soldiers pushed against each other, tripping over their comrades in their haste to get away.

Screams of panic and pain were drowned in the clatter of musketry as the Union infantry poured a devastating fire into the retreating Confederates. Sergeant Matthewson went down. A bullet had smashed his knee. Private Guthries was caught in the line of musket fire, and disappeared from the retreating tide. Breaking toward the rear, Tod tripped over a private from the next company who fell dead in front of him. Glancing over his shoulder, Duane saw a burly Union trooper grab up General Archer as others encircled and captured several dozen more. The enemy leveled their weapons and fired into the retreating mass.

"I'm hit!" Griffin screamed as he fell against Duane, knocking them both to the ground.

"Hurry!" Colonel Fry called. "Fall back across the stream!"

"Give em cover!" Lieutenant Jenkins ordered. "Load and fire on the run!"

A handful of Company K's troopers raised their muskets and fired on the advancing enemy. Crawling to his feet, Duane picked up his musket and found it empty as a Federal soldier charged with bayonet. Grabbing his weapon by the muzzle, he swung the butt against the gleaming blade. The attacker lost his grip as the musket fell from his grasp. Duane took advantage of his brief reprieve to help Tod to his feet.

"Here, take my musket an hold em if ya kin!" Duane shoved the weapon into his friend's hands and stooped to help Howard.

Tod jammed the drumsticks into his belt and slung the drum around behind his back as he knelt to reload the gun. In the surge of action, the men of the regiment broke into a wild route as the enemy continued their heavy fire and began to round up prisoners. Howard was bleeding from a head wound and temporarily disoriented in the roar of battle.

"Look out!" Tod warned.

Pushing his wounded comrade toward the drummer boy, Duane drew his revolver. "Hurry, Tod! Help Howard!"

Tod grabbed the corporal as the boy and his enemy fired at each other, and the random firing about the battlefield continued to take its toll. Neither of the two was hit. Duane fired again to stop the oncoming bayonet. His bullet tore through the arm of the attacking trooper, its force spinning him off his feet. The boy kept his revolver ready as he hurried to help Tod to assist their wounded friend toward the rear. The first soldier had recovered his weapon and was once again on the offensive. Before the boy could react, a shell exploded behind the enemy soldier and ripped him to pieces. Fragments of the shell whizzed through the underbrush as one ripped through Tod's shirt, cutting a gash in his side.

"Damn!" the drummer boy cried. He dropped the musket, fell to his knees, and pressed his hands to the wound.

The blood flowed fast and soaked between his fingers as the corporal tumbled into the grass and Duane hurried to his aid.

"Ya bad hurt?" Duane asked as he glanced first at the flow of blood and then toward the action around them.

"Ain't knowin," Tod's voice quavered. "Cain't feel no pain yet."

Gunfire continued all around the slope and men continued to retreat in the rush of the oncoming Federal infantrymen.

"We gotta git 'r we's gonna be taken," Duane advised.

"Ya gotta git without me," Howard instructed. "I cain't see right 'r move straight an'll only slow ya down."

"We gotta try enyhow," Duane replied.

"Dee's right," Tod agreed. "I'm okay. Ya jest hang on the two a us."

The boys helped the youthful corporal to his feet and the three moved away, keeping low to the ground. The air was filled with the pulsating sound and motion of the murderous conflict. Caught up in the midst of retreating infantrymen, the three soon found themselves splashing through the creek toward a small stand of trees in a bend in the water's course. Suddenly Tod collapsed bringing the others stumbling to the ground.

"Sorry," the boy apologized. "My legs give out."

Duane saw the bleeding had soaked through a large area of the drummer boy's shirt and waistband.

"We ain't goin no fu'th'r," he stated. "Ya needs tendin' an this tree stand's as good cover as we kin git."

"Ya look like death," Howard observed. "How bad's it look, Dee?"

"Better 'n the last time he was hit. Jest needs bandagin' fer the present an safe passage ta friendly territory fer some rest."

The three were not alone in their piece of woodlot. Several other dead and wounded lay about the underbrush. Some moaned for water or wept at their fate or the loss of a friend. Some lay conscious in the last moments before death would take them. One mumbled to himself in a state of shock while another sat against a tree gazing at the bloodied ground.

Outside the relative quiet of the trees, the battle was subsiding. Elements of the Confederate brigade had established a skirmish line along the fence on the west side of the meandering run. The Federals were herding their prisoners up the slope to the back of the ridge. More troops and artillery were forming along the ridge as the cavalry was relieved. The remnants of Archer's brigade had retreated to the opposite ridge where a new Confederate offensive was being prepared.

Over the next hour, Duane tended first to Tod and Howard, then, with Griffin's help, did what he could to comfort others nearby. Fabric for bandages and a flask of brandy were rummaged from the victims scattered about the ground. Dressings were fashioned from a linen shirt found in a haversack, soaked with the brandy, then secured in place by fabric strips ripped from another spare shirt. Water was shared from canteens taken from the dead or carried by the living.

The noise of activity from the Federal lines and from the skirmishers, firing along the fence, served to mask any noise or movement from Duane and his comrades. Their position was near the edge of a no-man's land, and no one seemed interested in their small piece of territory.

Once settled medically, Duane and Howard turned their attention to securing weapons and ammunition and to seeing to Tod's safety. A slightly wounded sergeant was helped to a safer position as well. Both were tucked as comfortably as possible alongside a fallen and partially rotted tree trunk, where it was hoped they would be protected from shell fragments and bullets. The drum, unhooked from its strap, was likewise set along the fallen trunk. There was nothing more to do but wait and watch. For the corporal, time was its own medicine. The longer they waited, the better he felt.

The skirmishers sniped at the Union regiments taking position about four hundred yards beyond the creek and up the slope. But their activity was brought to an abrupt end when the Federals sent out their own companies of skirmishers to charge down the slope and force the Rebels to beat a hasty retreat to Herr's Ridge.

Duane and his comrades could see their own brigades forming in the open fields near the tavern. In a short time, they moved out of enemy fire and into a thin line of trees that edged the top of the slope, starting a quarter mile back from the road. As the three watched, two brigades of General Hill's corps spread out amongst the trees, the first in a fairly straight line of regiments

101

shoulder to shoulder and the second in echelon—stepped by regiments with each off the front right corner of the other.

The Federal forces were moving into three lines of battle with the first along the thickets bordering the stream, the second part way up the slope, and the third near the crest. They spread from the road, through the wood lot in the middle, to the fields beyond the woods. A battery of artillery was added to the middle of the Union left.

In the valley between the ridges there was a brick farm house and a barn with a wheat field out behind. The fugitives watched as the grand action during the midday lull consisted of Federal sharpshooters occupying the farm to snipe at the Confederates, and a Confederate company's sweep to drive off the sharpshooters. Otherwise, the day was marked by some long-range artillery exchanges to feel out each other's positions.

"Ya think ther'll be eny action?" Tod whispered.

"Should be," Griffin responded. "The lines keep buildin' so somethin's gotta happen. We jest gotta lay low so's them Yanks don't come at us."

A crashing was heard in the underbrush and voices approached.

"Play dead," the wounded sergeant instructed. "They's too busy gittin' ready fer an attack ta give eny notice ta dead 'r wounded layin' 'bout."

Duane and Howard had both loaded their weapons and were prepared for battle should it come to them. They quietly eased themselves to the ground, stretching prone alongside a rock and the root structure of a tree. Duane covered his revolver with leaves and rested his hand overtop of it. Howard lay his musket snugly along the edge of a fallen tree limb. The voices came closer. A small group of Federal skirmishers walked past the wounded toward the edge of the tree stand near the wheat field. There they took position using the trees for cover, and awaited the inevitable attack. Numbering a half dozen, they were well-disciplined, for once in place, they settled quietly with only soft whispers between them. Duane and his companions remained silent. Each knew he must not make a sound or a move.

Waiting seemed forever. The day had become hot and sultry, though the midday heat was blessedly relieved by the shade of the trees.

At noon, the waiting was interrupted by the distant booming of artillery. A moment later, shells could be heard screaming over the road near the farmhouse on the ridge, and crashing about the fields. A new Confederate position about a mile to the north had begun to bombard the Federals.

It should be soon, Duane thought. But the waiting continued.

The distant artillery fired for over an hour. It was followed by distant sounds of a growing battle. Still nothing had happened in the immediate area except for the shouting of orders amidst exploding shells up near the farmhouse, and the rearranging of Federal brigades along the road.

Another hour passed.

"They're getting ready," a Union skirmisher told his comrades.

Duane looked toward the ridge. The regiments were dressing on their flags and preparing to attack. Federal musketry and cannon opened the instant the Confederate line stepped from the trees, but their aim was high and ineffective. What a grand sight, the boy thought as he watched the elements of his corps step off and advance down the hill.

There was a quarter mile to cover. Once on the move, the Rebel brigades opened fire on the skirmishers and the underbrush along the stream. Bullets ripped through the thickets, tearing at the trees and shrubs. Some dug up the ground in small puffs of dust. Duane prayed that a merciful God would protect them from a stray bullet. Within minutes, the Confederate regiments had swung into a single line of battle and were sweeping across the bottom land through meadow and wheat field as they approached the underbrush along the run.

The skirmishers pulled back toward the stream, joined by dozens more who had moved into their positions from either side, unseen by the Confederate refugees remaining motionless on the ground. The air suddenly erupted with the scream of demons as the attacking regiments advanced in order through the thickets along the waterway and reformed on the far side. Caught up in the surge of advancing troops, Duane and Howard found themselves swept forward in the disciplined ranks of a North Carolina regiment. They went with the knowledge that neither the sergeant nor Tod was critical and would be safe in each other's care.

Erupting in full fury, the battle was joined at about twenty yards with each army pouring a continuous withering fire into the other. The Carolinians fought with disciplined determination as their ranks were pounded by artillery on the right and were wickedly cut down by a raking musketry to the front. Bullets filled the air with their deadly buzzing and whined off rocks and trees. As the front line of Confederate infantrymen was shattered, those still standing formed immediately on their silken banner and continued to press the attack.

The color bearer fell dead and another rushed forward to lift the flag. He, too, was immediately shot. In seconds a third was killed instantly. Still the regiment reformed and held its center. The right end of the brigade advanced in the fields along the back side of the woodlot while the rest worked its way through the trees. Artillery fire had taken out an entire company on the right leaving but two or three of its members in the fight. Duane and Howard moved through the woods, firing from trees where they could. Muskets and rifles scythed down ranks of attacking troops as they fired in line. Splinters filled the air from trees and rifle butts to tear through flesh and clothing. Shrieks of agony mixed with the whine of bullets and the thunderclaps of exploding shells. Smoke-filled air stung the eyes and burned the lungs. The elements of the two armies continued to clash at short range—standing, shooting, falling, dying, reloading, and shooting again. Another color bearer went down and a young colonel took the flag. A soldier rushed to relieve his colonel of the bloodied banner and both went down in the hail of lead. All about the surge of movement shifted in constant motion. A lieutenant colonel knelt beside his regimental commander for a moment, then pulled the blood-soaked silk from beneath the officer and waved it high. A lieutenant tried to stop him.

"Twenty-sixth, follow me!" he called, then collapsed from a bullet through his head.

A severe slaughter had covered the wooded landscape in the space of forty minutes with a carpet of over a thousand dead and wounded. The men of the North Carolina regiment filled the air with their wild yelling and a fresh hail of lead, and their enemy fled. They surged forward and the fight advanced halfway up the wooded hill.

Wrapped in the concussion of battle, pounding at every nerve and smothering the senses and the brain in a dull blanket of reflex action, Duane advanced with the tide. His clothing had been torn by flying debris, and soiled from the dust and dirt of battle, the sweat of his own body and the life-blood spewed from those struck down at close range. The boy had emptied his revolver in the early minutes of the battle and holstered it for a rifle off the ground. Kneeling beside a wounded soldier, he leveled the weapon at a figure in blue. Squeezing the trigger, he saw through the smoke, the impact of his bullet as the man fell back, grabbing at his shattered leg.

Still the air hummed with flying lead and roared with the explosive musketry. There was a sudden impact in his side and a surge of pain as he fell back and was struck by the heel of a passing soldier's shoe. A short distance away in the movement of grey, Howard went down as a bullet tore through his chest and erupted in red.

The second line of battle gave way and the attack moved to the crest of the wooded slope. The boy and his companion found themselves near one another as the din of battle moved forward.

"Ya hurt bad?" Duane asked.

"Yea," his friend answered. "Tell em as I died facin' the enemy."

He was gone.

Duane looked to see where he'd been hit and found the bullet had passed through his cartridge pouch and lodged in the leather of his belt. The boy found another musket and ammunition and moved forward to join the battle. The thought never entered his mind that he could stay where he was and no one would care.

The conflict had moved to the crest of the ridge, but few remained of the original combatants from either army. For more than an hour, the fight had been fought as the brigades of two armies had destroyed each other. Fresh troops charged across the little valley and roared up the ridge in a new wave of grey. The enemy broke and fled to another ridge, a short distance beyond where a school building stood. The remaining men of the North Carolina regiment were out of ammunition. They paused to resupply themselves from the dead and wounded as fresh brigades took up the fight, then hurried to follow with them.

Duane glanced about him as he stood with his own new supply of cartridges, and saw that the rest of the exhausted remnants of the leading brigades had been relieved of further combat. He went no further, deciding instead to retrace his journey and check on Tod and the sergeant.

*　　*　　*

Cool evening breezes drifted up the slopes of the ridge, wafting off the waters of Willoughby Run. Duane, Tod, and others from the company worked their way through the thickets along the run to begin the grim task of gathering the dead and to help the remaining wounded as best they could. It was three hours since the Union line had broken from the top of the ridge. The distant sounds of battle continued along the heights on the far side of town. Here in these fields and woods the cries and moans of the wounded begged for water or help or the peace of death. Some called to God. Some called for their mothers. Thousands of broken and bloodied men and boys lay scattered on the battle-torn and blood-reddened landscape. The slaughter of the afternoon had been beyond belief. Nearly three quarters of all who had fought on the wooded acres had fallen.

"Oh, God!" Lieutenant Jenkins whispered. "If only those who sit in capitols of countries would walk this field an see their families slaughtered as these are."

"I really don't figger they'd do no differ'nt," Sergeant Raymond commented. "Let's do as we kin fer these poor souls."

Bearing litters from the ambulance wagons, the small company began to work their way up the slope.

"The battlefield robbers've already bin here," Tod observed. "Shoes 'n gear is already gone."

"Yeh," Duane agreed. "Seein' as I picked up thin's fer us an others musta done the same."

"Water," a whisper of a voice begged.

"Right here," Private Matthewson responded.

Fifteen-year-old Jamie Matthewson knelt by a wounded soldier to offer his canteen. Sergeant Raymond joined him to help place the ragged soldier onto a stretcher. The others moved on. By two's and three's they dropped aside to help the wounded or to gather the dead from the company.

The wounded were the first order of business except for those dead whose friends had come to gather the remains. Across the acres of McPherson's farm, the bandsmen, survivors, and capable wounded worked among the fallen.

Duane and Tod had decided that their first effort would be to locate Matthew Guthries. They knew he had fallen in the morning retreat, but had no idea as to how badly he'd been hurt.

"Over here!" Corporal Doherty called. "It's Matthew an he's alive!"

They rushed to a spot in the open field where the corporal knelt.

"Sher am glad ta see ya all," Matthew smiled weakly. "It's bin a hell of a day, lyin round an wond'rin if someone would git me fer the fight could end."

"How'd ya make it?" Duane asked.

"God's own luck, Dee. This poor Yankee boy weren't thet bad off. A stray bullet caught him in the back. He knew he was goin an told me 'bout his mama. It were damned pitiful as he couldn't go quick, but lingered with his back broke fer more'n an hour."

"Where ya hit?" Cameron asked.

"First one got ma foot. Then I took one in the hand, another in the leg, an a few scratches 'bout. The real devil is ma arm. I think it's pretty much tore up by a shell piece."

"Ain't at all pretty," a bandsman commented as he approached bearing a litter. "Ya kin load him on an me 'n Theo, here'll take him ta the hospital."

"Thanks," Corporal Dougherty acknowledged.

The wounded teenager was eased onto the stretcher to begin his journey back to health. The corporal and the boys moved on.

"I wanna git Howard," Duane stated. "Somewhere's in them woods. I think he's dead."

"Ya take us ther," Tod said.

Stepping carefully among the carpet of corpses and wounded, the three walked to the woods in the center of the ridge's slope. Blackened by powder smoke and dirt, the shattered bodies made footing difficult as they lay so thick about the grassy landscape made slippery from its coat of blood.

McPherson's woods was a horror all its own. Trees and vegetation had been splintered and shredded by artillery and rifle shot. Their debris blended with such a compressed volume of casualties that the mix of blue and grey fabric with green and brown vegetation splashed everywhere with red and gore caused even the stoutest of men and boys to sicken at the sight.

Duane had been there before with the frozen dead at Murfreesboro. Tod was seeing it for the first time. His stomach retched and convulsed as he became sick without warning and began to cough and vomit. His head began to swim in dizzy confusion. Badly shaken, he collapsed to his hands and knees. The smell of gore and death was as a great cloud that completely enveloped the senses and twisted the boy's insides beyond description. The corporal was also paralyzed with illness as Duane, too, fought to keep from losing control.

Finally, the boy and the young man were able to help the drummer boy up to lean against a scarred tree.

"Oh, God, Dee," he spit the vomit from his mouth and wiped his face with his sleeve, as his voice shook with sobs and his body convulsed with uncontrolled emotion. The violent racking tore open his wound and he grabbed suddenly at his side as pain seared his mind. "No!" he screamed. His blood seeped through the bandage and clothing to escape between his fingers.

"Hurry!" Cameron reached to steady the boy as he lost consciousness and slipped to the ground. "Git some one ta help Tod!"

"We're comin!" It was Foley. He and Kim had followed into the woods when the sergeant had informed them that he had seen Tod headed in that direction with the others.

"What happened?" Kim asked, choking in the stench.

"The sight a this place made him so sick he hurt his self," Cameron explained.

"Why'd ya come in here?" Foley asked. Anger tinged his voice.

"Dee was takin us ta git Griffin's body," the corporal explained.

"Ya stay with Tod," the youth ordered. "We'll go with Dee."

Corporal Howard Griffin's body was located near the middle of the woodlot. The stiffness of death had begun to set in as it was lifted onto a stretcher for removal from the battleground.

"Dee, we'll take the body," Kim said, his voice edged in anger. "Ya help Cameron git Tod back ta the camp an tend ta gittin him fixed proper ta healin. An ya stay's there, hear! I ain't wantin either a ya out on this death place no more!"

"I'll do as ya says, Kim. But don't ya be takin it out on me." Duane's voice broke as deep hurt and emotion tightened in his throat. "We're all in this war of the same army. He's hurtin cause we're soldiers in the fightin. It ain't my doin!"

Foley reached for the sobbing boy and pulled him into his arms. "I'm sorry, Dee. God, I'm sorry," he cried. The older youth's tears rolled off his cheeks and fell wet in the boy's hair.

The two stood for a moment, locked in a caring and hurt-filled embrace, their tears damp on each other's body. The three wept quietly as Kim wrapped his arms around the first two. For a long moment neither spoke.

All about the woods, the living worked to care for the fallen as the cousins sent Duane to take care of their nephew while they took their burden to be buried.

*   *   *

General Heth's division had gone into camp on the back side of Herr's Ridge. The survivors of the day's fighting were exhausted as they lounged about their camp. Many remained out on the other side of the run, on the slopes of McPherson's Ridge, helping the bandsmen and other non-combatants to bring in the dead and wounded. Hospitals had been set up in nearby buildings or in tents at the edge of the camp. The cries and moans of the wounded in the field were joined by the screams of pain and the pleadings of those on the surgeons' tables. It was a night of pain, of sadness, of mourning. The stench of death rankled the air as beasts, slaughtered in the battle, rotted on the fields or roads. Burning cookfires scented the air, lanterns cast their faint circles of light, soft conversation carried on the breeze. The rattle of wagons and artillery, the march of infantry, passed along the pike and other distant roads, as the elements of the Army of Northern Virginia continued to gather from points north and west.

General Lee had moved ahead to the ridge closer to the town and stretching south from the seminary school that Duane had seen from the edge of the woods wherein he had fought. General

110

Longstreet had joined him there and located parts of his corps along that ridge. Others from General Ewell's corps were camped to the north of the town. The Union Army had taken position on the far side of Gettysburg along the cemetery heights. The day's fighting ended after nightfall with sounds of battle far distant from the slaughter in farmer McPherson's fields and woodlot.

Duane had returned to the encampment with Tod and Cameron. Tod's wound had been cleaned and redressed and he had been settled in his tent to rest. Kim and Foley had gone on to a field across the pike where several of the dead had been buried. Corporal Griffin was laid to rest in an unmarked grave twenty paces due north of a sycamore tree. Foley had made a map of the grave's location in case his family would want to move the remains home after the war.

Daylight had gone as night crept on with a clear sky and a brilliant sparkle of starlight. Duane sat by the fire with Kim and Foley. Tod lay on his blankets under his shelter tent, chin resting atop his clasped hands. His drum lay back near his feet. The coffee pot contained boiling water and the cylinders from the revolver. In addition, Duane had brought back, with the help of Tod and the wounded sergeant, another revolver and full gear along with two rifled muskets, cartridges, and caps.

"This how it's done?" Foley asked as he worked to clean a spare cylinder.

"Thet's the hang of it," the boy affirmed, busy wiping down the revolver.

"Yer sher gonna be in good shape, Tod," Kim stated. "Dee here's seen ta it ya kin carry a gun jest in case ya cain't git em with yer sticks 'n drum."

The four chuckled at the thought.

"Sher do thank ya fer gittin me back in one piece," Tod commented. "Sorry I went sick on ya in the woods."

"Cain't think a not havin a tent partner," Duane replied. "'Sides, if ya weren't here I'd have ta drum an it'd be certain as I'd be shot fer messin up the beat."

111

Another bit of laughter rippled from the gathering.

Others of the company were gathered in quiet groups, reliving the events of the day, sharing stories or news they'd gathered along the way, and telling of the horrors they had witnessed while helping the wounded. As the night deepened and some of the exhausted slept, others lay awake, conversed with friends, or continued to help in the field. Activity of the litter brigades and the burial parties continued through the night. There were some who settled by a fire in the wee hours of the morning to write a letter to the family of a friend who had been killed.

Duane and his friends finished cleaning the guns and reloading the cylinders. The weapons were set aside, the coffee pot rinsed out, and a pot of coffee brewed. As it cooked along, Foley worked in the dimness of the firelight to write a letter home to the Griffin family. The night wore on to midnight. The four stayed near each other, shared hot cups of coffee, wrapped their blankets across their shoulders, and lay down by the fire. Drifting in and out of sleep, they listened to the insects of the night, the distant dogs, the lowing cattle. Somewhere a cock crowed, disoriented by the day's events.

Eventually, the weight of exhaustion took over and soft snoring drifted on the night air.

*   *   *

Thursday dawned quietly. Roosters crowed in the predawn glow. Black crows cawed raucously at the intruders who inhabited the countryside. The soldiers were called to muster as the camps came awake. Their ranks had been drastically thinned by the losses of the previous day's fighting. Fires were rekindled and breakfast of biscuit and salted meat was cooked. Those who had it, boiled coffee.

The morning wore on quietly. Some of the regiments were entertained by their bands who attempted to raise their spirits with music.

General Heth had been wounded during the afternoon assault in which so many had perished, and General Pettigrew had assumed command. General Hill had sent his division under General Anderson to the front. Pettigrew's brigades would be held in reserve for the day. But the day continued to pass quietly as the temperature climbed into the 80s and the weary soldiers sought relief from the sultry heat in the shade of their tents. But even the tents were like ovens as the sun radiated through the canvass.

In the late afternoon, the battle erupted to the south with the thunder of artillery. As the batteries of Hill's corps added their firepower to the storm, the air shook and the ground trembled. For the men on Herr's Ridge, the fight was far away. They hoped their comrades would succeed in beating the enemy, but they knew it would not happen.

The men of Company K gathered for evening muster. They felt the loss of their thinned ranks as the role was called and they looked about where friends and comrades had been. The company broke for supper. The evening wore dark, and the bugler called the soldiers to their beds.

Duane awoke sometime after midnight, restless in anticipation of more battle yet to come. A brilliant moon, just past full, illuminated the sleeping camps. Unable to sleep, the boy crawled from his bed and wandered to the crest of the ridge. There he stood and gazed about the softly lit landscape. Shattered buildings and the shell-torn woods and fields lay bathed in quiet brilliance. Gettysburg's silhouette stood crisp in the distance. The town clock struck three in the morning. As the boy turned to go back to his bed he heard the creak of wagons. As a farm boy it sounded like hay rigs off to an early start. As a soldier he knew it to be artillery being set in place for the coming day's work.

Duane wandered back to the tent. Glancing once more along the line, he gazed for a moment at his comrades, asleep in their field tents, bathed gently by soft moonlight. The boy lowered himself to the ground, crawled beneath the canvass roof, and wrapped himself in his blanket. Pillowing his head on his outstretched arm, he soon drifted back to sleep.

*   *   *

The moon had passed far toward the western horizon, casting long shadows in the soft light edged with dawn. It caressed the dark tangles of hair of drummer boy and tentmate. The two stirred. Tod lifted his head to gaze out in the predawn light as Duane rolled over and opened his eyes. The older boy propped his chin in the palms of his hands. There was movement in the camp as officers were about, talking in small knots, then moving on.

"Hi," Duane greeted.

"Cain't sleep," Tod returned.

The two lay awake, listening to the morning sounds of distant farms and nearby birds. An incessant chatter in the tree tops greeted an approaching dawn as robins and sparrows flitted about and blue jays called to each other.

"They sher sounds perty," Tod stated.

"Wish I was in ma bed back home an this war 'd never come," Duane added. "This sounds like ar farm back home, so full a peace 'n perty bird song."

Suddenly a deep booming erupted in the distance as artillery fired on the heights beyond the town. The boys both shook as the unexpected concussion startled them. The air quickly exploded into a continuous thunder of cannon as the first fighting of the day got underway.

"They's sher as hell got a early start," Tod commented.

"Reckon we best git to," Duane suggested. "Muster cain't be far off."

The boys sat up and pulled their shoes on, then packed their blankets. Before they finished, Willis was by to pass the word for muster.

"How's the bandage doin?" Duane asked as the older boy slipped the drum strap over his head.

"Still holdin," Tod replied. "Feels a bit wet from seepin'. But I think it's started ta scab ov'r."

The two stepped out and Tod hooked the drum to its strap. Duane glanced at his friend's shirt to be sure there was no significant bleeding. He sure must be running on nerves and energy, Duane thought. The blood he'd lost should have put him out of action.

The two proceeded to Lieutenant Jenkin's tent and sounded the muster roll.

Once the company had gathered, the lieutenant gave the men their instructions. "Cook yer breakfast 'n pack yer gear. Fill yer canteens. We move in an hour."

"What's happenin', Lieutenant?" Corporal DiPhilippo asked.

"We're movin up ta the Seminary ridge inta the line a battle ta wait further orders."

The men were dismissed to eat and strike their camp. Throughout the early hours of sunrise and camp activity, the distant fighting continued. Artillery was mixed with rifle fire. The shout of orders and the yelling of charging brigades, drifted on the quiet air. As the sun rose on the new day, so also did the temperature and the humidity. It would be another sultry July day.

"Think we'll be seein' action?" Jamie asked as he passed Duane and Tod in route from filling canteens at the stream.

"We has ta," Tod answered, rolling his tent half to tie into his field pack. "We rested yestaday an' ever'one else was fightin'."

"May be as the fightin' goin' now'll end it all," Duane put in hopefully.

"Ya know's it ain't ta be," Tod said flatly.

"Yeh."

"I ain't sher I kin go inta 'nother fight," Jamie whispered staring at the ground. "It ain't thet I's a coward," he looked at the two boys, not much younger then himself. "It's jest as I'm all a quiverin' inside 'n ain't got maself t'gether yet from the fightin' day b'fer."

"Jamie, ya ain't gotta tell us. We was ther 'n as feels much the same," Tod comforted.

Sergeant Henson approached the three boys.

"Call the muster, Tod." he instructed.

"Let's go," the boy stated.

The three walked together to where the company's headquarters had been. There Tod sounded the roll and the men began to gather.

Across the open ground of the ridge, the camps had been struck and the companies were assembling. As elsewhere, their commanding officers were giving out instructions for the next movement.

"We're gonna be part of a major offensive on the center of the enemy's line," Jenkins was saying. "Ev'ry able man is goin' with us. Thet includes wounded who kin fight and camp staff, too. So, Willis, ya be sher ya has a gun fer with ta shoot those people."

"I sherly will, Mass'r Jenkins."

"We move inta place quiet-like an out a the enemy's sight," the lieutenant continued. "Thet means no cherrin' and no drum, Tod."

"Yes, Sir, Lieutenant," the boy acknowledged.

It was early morning, yet, when the division started down the road, then across the fields to the back side of Seminary Ridge. All along the crest of the high ground, the troops saw the lines of artillery. Duane counted over four dozen varying pieces as the brigade moved quietly to its position. Across the shallow valley, a little more than a mile away, the fighting continued. From their position below the line of sight, the moving soldiers could not see the panoramic view, only the high thick cloud of smoke which hung above the battle.

Colonel Fry took his regiments to the back side of a wooded line. There they moved into the shade of the trees and were ordered to lie down, keep quiet—no cheers, and keep low. General Pettigrew checked the positioning of the troops in the division. He had assumed command in the absence of the wounded Heth. His brigade, in turn, was commanded by Colonel

Marshall and placed in line to the left of Colonel Fry's brigade. About a quarter mile through the woods, to the right was the left of General Pickett's division, just arrived on the battlefield. Thus, Company K was near the edge of a large gap between two lines of assault which would later unite to become the center of the advancing charge.

General Lee and Lieutenant-General Longstreet rode by to inspect the preparations. Knowing they could not cheer their general, the men raised their hats instead. He acknowledged them as he moved along, conversing with various division commanders along the way.

"Many of these poor boys should go to the rear," he was overheard to say. "They are not fit for duty."

Duane glanced about from where he sat beside Tod. There were a lot of men and boys with filthy wrappings of bandages to cover wounds of varying severity. Some of the men sat in small groups to talk. Others stretched out and slept. Some quenched their thirst or munched on a biscuit. A few stood, too nervous to remain in one place. And a couple here and there wandered toward the front to gaze through the trees at the lay of the land and the enemy lines.

"I'm goin up ta take a look," Duane told his friend.

"I think I'll stay put," Tod said. "Tell me what ya see."

"I'll go with ya," Foley offered.

The two walked through the mass of troops to the front edge of the trees. There they stood to gaze about the gentle roll of farm and fields and the battle line beyond. From their vantage point they saw where the woods extended to a point at their right and a fence line continued beyond. A road traversed the center open ground running across at an angle from left to right. Smoke continued to roll up from a distant hill to the left and the cannon flashes could be seen near the ground. The spang from the smooth-bore guns was distinctly different from the slap of the rifled guns as the sound carried in distorted delay over the distance between flash and concussion.

"Look!" Foley pointed to a barn near the road in front of where they stood.

An advancing wave of blue charged across from a stone fence and attacked the barn. There was an exchange of musketry, clearly distinct on the morning air, as the white puffs of discharge popped out from the wooden wall of the barn and the rifles of the soldiers in blue. A new sound erupted suddenly from the woods to the left as a battery of guns fired on the Union attackers. The exchange was brief. In a few short minutes, Confederate sharpshooters were retreating to their battle line while the troops in blue streamed back toward their fence, leaving the barn ablaze and of no further use to anyone.

Colonel Fry approached from the side. For a moment he watched quietly with the boy and the youth from his command. The sound of distant battle continued to rise and fall as the tide of the sea.

"See that clump a trees," he finally spoke. "The one near the angle in that stone wall." He pointed to a spot in the center of the Union line where the ridge was low and almost indistinct and the fields rose in a broad and gentle sweep. The two nodded. "That's where we're headed," the colonel explained. "Just now I'm on my way ta see General Pickett ta be sure that we meet out there before we get to the enemy."

"Would be a good idea," Foley grinned. "It'll be hell ta go it alone."

The colonel agreed, then continued on his way as Duane and Foley took one last look before returning to their company. There, along the fence at the point of woods, they saw a lone figure sitting and gazing sadly across the farm lands. It was General Longstreet.

As the sun climbed toward noon, the distant fighting ended suddenly. A quiet hung over the battlefield. Hardly a breeze stirred. The fields outside the woods radiated waves of heat as the temperature soared through the eighties. The woods offered little relief. There was little movement or breeze to cut away the stuffy staleness in the air. The soldiers had consumed their water and lay in extreme discomfort.

During the hours of waiting, the generals continued to ride the line and inspect the disposition of infantry and artillery. Maximum supplies of ammunition were placed by the guns. The generals met with their division commanders who met with their brigade commanders who met with their regimental commanders who met with their company commanders who met with their men. Every detail of the intended charge was explained to the men. There would be an artillery bombardment first to soften the enemy line and to destroy their artillery or drive it from the field. Then the charge would follow. There would be no Rebel yell or quickstep until the very last moment. They would advance in perfect order until they reached the enemy line of fire. The men knew what was expected. It was time to send out the skirmishers to clear the way and to break down the fence lines.

Quiet continued through the middle of the day. The skirmishers went forward to prepare the way. Among the members of Company K on skirmisher assignment, was Corporal Doherty. The wait continued. The artillery was to begin its work at 1:30 sharp. The men checked with a friend who had a watch, and waited.

"Everybody down," Sergeant Raymond finally ordered.

There was an anxious moment of silence. Then to the far right, a cannon fired. A moment later, a second gun fired. Suddenly, a crescendo erupted in steadily increasing intensity sweeping from right to left as a hundred and forty guns exploded into action. A great cloud of smoke rolled up about the batteries and drifted into the woods. The roar of cannon continued as the ground shook and the air vibrated from the constant concussion of sound. It rose and fell in waves as batteries paused here and there to reload and fire in salvo.

Duane held his hands to his ears as he flattened himself as low to the ground as his empty stomach would allow. At the first sound of the guns, a rabbit had scurried from the underbrush as flocks of birds took flight from the treetops. Tod had called after the rabbit.

"Git along ya little rabbit. I'd be gittin, too, if'n I was a rabbit like ya!"

Then he, too, had flattened out with his hands over his ears.

Roaring cannons shook the ground and the air with a violence greater than an erupting volcano. A vicious rain of death and destruction poured forth against the Federal lines. All about had become one constant and continuous explosion of sound with such intensity as to press against the nerves and bodies of the thousands lying in readiness along the woods, like some great weight from heaven above. The concussion of cannon continued unchanged for fifteen minutes.

Suddenly there was a horrendous crashing through the trees above joined by the whir and whine of enemy shells raining through the woods. Shells exploded in the air and amidst the massed troops on the ground. As tree limbs and shrapnel rained down from above, blankets, packs, and human flesh erupted in flashes of flames from the ground. Cries of "We have wounded!" mixed with the screams and moans of injured and dying infantrymen. Chaos broke lose as officers warned "Keep down!" and tried to calm their troops. Duane could hear the rip of flying shell fragments and the whump of solid shot as the rain of death and destruction continued all about.

A shell exploded nearby killing Corporal DiPhilippo and two others as it wounded a half dozen more. Colonel Fry was struck in the shoulder by a fragment of shell. Another hit close and Duane could hear it clearly as it sliced through fabric and flesh.

"Ahhh!" Tod screamed in pain.

The younger boy turned quickly to see what he could do. Tod lay on the ground, shaking violently in shock and pain as blood pooled beneath his leg. A portion of flesh had been ripped away from the calf of his leg along with the fabric of his trousers. A ragged hole of shredded tissue and muscle poured forth its flow of blood.

"Ya ain't dyin'!" Duane screamed at his friend. "Gimme a shirt from yer pack!"

While the air about rained its deadly storm of destruction and the ground continued to quake with the cannonade, Duane worked to wrap Tod's wound to hold until he could get to a surgeon. The drummer boy calmed as fear was replaced by pain.

"I cain't be there," he sobbed. "The company won't have a drum beat fer the march."

"I kin do fer ya," Duane assured. "Let me have the drum."

The drum's skin head hummed in the intensity of noise and vibration of air as the artillery fire continued for an hour and a half. When it finally ended, and the guns were quiet, it felt as though such a weight had been lifted that Duane sensed a light-headedness and a feeling of floating in air. Tod lay where he had been when struck by the piece of shell. The wound had been wrapped with a shirt. Duane sat beside him. The drum was strapped in place. He was ready to beat the cadence for his friend.

"Here," Tod offered his revolver. "Ya'll need this mor'n me, now."

"I'll do fine with jest mine," Duane smiled. "I's seen where we're ta go. It ain't likely I'll come back."

"Oh, God, no!" Tod gasped. But he saw in his friend's eyes that he believed it to be so. "Ya gotta come back," the wounded boy said. "Ya jest gotta."

"Form up," Lieutenant Jenkins ordered.

"Ya take care," Duane said as he stood to leave.

"Ya do the same," Tod waved.

As the troops formed in ranks and prepared to move out, there remained in their shell-torn waiting area more than three hundred dead and wounded who could not go along.

Tod watched the company take its place with the regiment. The regimental flag moved to its place in front as the companies dressed on their banner and straightened their ranks. Company K set its two files with Duane and Lieutenant Jenkins on the front right corner. The remaining officers followed behind to keep the files closed and to discourage any who might prefer to flee.

"Forward. Guide Center. March!"

The cadence was struck. The brigade advanced into the sunlight.

Tears streamed down Tod's cheeks as he watched his friend go forth to an uncertain fate. Duane's face, too, was moist with tears as he thought of the friend whose drum he beat and the possibility that this could be the last event in his life. He pushed these thoughts from his mind, straightened erect, and felt a surge of pride as he glanced along the line of men and flags.

*   *   *

The 13th Alabama regiment advanced to the right of center. The 1st Tennessee held the right end of the line. The remaining three regiments stretched to the left. Duane saw only one other brigade clear the woods with Fry's. It was Pettigrew's. General Pettigrew appeared concerned that the remaining brigades on the left were not advancing. Finally they appeared and the whole line was dressed and in straight order as it neared the end of the point of wood to the right.

Duane continued to keep the cadence—a hundred and ten steps per minute for a forward rate of just under a hundred yards per minute. Looking ahead the boy saw clearly in the distance, beneath the rising smoke from the cannonade, the lines of blue defenders along walls and fences, and the clusters of artillery whose crews were busy preparing their guns. It certainly didn't appear that the artillery had done its job.

On either side of the road in front, were the thin lines of skirmishers, bobbing in wheat fields as they prepared to open fire on each other. They had been the safest during the artillery duel. The shells had simply traveled overhead.

The advancing line cleared the last trees and the boy could see the men of Pickett's division in the field a little ahead and far to the right. If he weren't so twisted in his gut by a deep-set fear, Duane might have seen something grand in the mile-wide front of brigades in dressed formation. But the distant puffs of smoke on the hilltops beyond the right and left were followed by the booming of artillery.

Still the line advanced. Artillery opened on both flanks and in places along the front. Shells screamed through the hot mid-afternoon air and exploded in the ranks. Pieces of bodies and gear blew into the air as the missiles of death took their toll. Great holes appeared in the ranks as ten men or more were taken out by a single shell. So far, the center of the line was relatively safe.

Pickett's division reached a stretch of low ground, out of the line of fire. There it paused to redress its lines. Moving forward once again, it came under a sudden and destructive fire. Then, on command, the whole division shifted to a left oblique and marched at a 45 degree angle. This slowed down the forward movement as it brought the entire division to the left to link with the end of Fry's line. The far left of Pettigrew's line collapsed under a flanking attack and began to fall back in disorderly retreat. The remaining brigades approached the road.

Because of the road's angle, the center of the line would strike it first. Colonel Fry's brigade was about two hundred and fifty yards from the Union line when the enemy fired in line by brigades and regiments. The impact of flying lead slammed into the front lines with devastating results. The flags went down, were picked back up, and continued forward. Scores of men fell wounded, some dead. Duane felt a sting of pain from a bullet that buzzed the side of his left leg. But it failed to slow him as another ripped through the wood of the drum. Artillery from several batteries opened with canister. All that the boy could see of the Federal front was a roiling cloud of smoke specked with flashes of fire in a long line.

"Forward!" Lieutenant Jenkins cried and waved his sword.

The companies advanced in bunches. Coming up against a board fence, the men of the brigade tried to break it down with their rifle butts. It would not give. The skirmishers before them had not been able to break down this section of fence. Here they waited and joined the line of attack. It would be necessary to go over the top.

As the first file crossed the top boards, sharpshooters opened fire. Foley was hit in the wrist but continued to advance. Duane heard a bullet whiz by his head and another strike the rim of the drum. Many slammed into the wooden planks and posts. Sergeant Henson was seriously wounded as a bullet passed through his neck and shoulder. He toppled into the ditch beside the roadway. Private Wilson was killed.

The line paused briefly in the safety of the roadway which ran below the grade of the field. The men lay down to rest a minute before going over the second fence on the opposite side of the road.

"I ain't wantin ta do this!" Jamie called to Duane over the roar of the battle.

"We're this far!" Duane called back. "Let's go finish it!"

They were on their feet again. Jamie slipped his rifle between the fence boards. Clambering over the planks as quickly as possible, they dropped to the ground on the other side amidst a hail of bullets, then rolled to their feet to go on.

Once past the fence, the lines redressed, linked up with Pickett's division, and moved forward as one solid front.

Enemy artillery and infantry continued heavy all along the front as the Confederate line closed and began its own destructive fire. The air was thick with cries of pain, the shout of orders, the whir and whine of lead. Great empty spaces continued to be blown in the Confederate ranks as artillery took out large numbers. The artillery back on Seminary Ridge continued to wreck havoc as its shells fell along the Union line and disabled men and cannon.

Officers were falling in great numbers as bullets and shell fragments found their marks. But still the colors remained upright and the remaining troops continued to close on them.

A slight grade remained before the Union fences. Colonel Fry led the charge as his little brigades swept furiously up the gentle slope. Firing and yelling, they flew forward. The colonel fell with a bullet in the thigh.

"Go on!" he called. "It will not last five minutes longer!"

To the right, the men from Pickett's left were with them. A lieutenant in a Virginia regiment clasped hands with a captain of the 1st Tennessee shouting, "Virginia and Tennessee will stand together on these works today!"

Both flanks of the Confederate line were being turned in. Duane felt the push of troops as they closed in on the center. Regimental colors were crowding into bunches as the men swarmed toward them. The low stone walls were only a few yards away. Now, for the first time since the lines stepped from the trees some twenty minutes back, the attackers let lose their blood-curdling Rebel yell and swept across the walls. Tennessians, Alabamians, and Virginians moved together.

Masses of blue ebbed about, trying to stay the attack. A few remaining artillerymen frantically loaded canister shot. Duane jammed his sticks into his belt and drew his revolver. A gun crew was loading to the right. He fired on one who went down. Others ran. The gun was turned. The boy fired again. In front, the Federals gave way in full retreat. The cannon fired its charge of canister into the flank of the Rebel mass. Screams of pain, cannon fire, muskets and rifles, the Rebel yell, shouts of orders, exploding shells pressed against the senses. The boy also felt a cutting pain as a shard from a shattered stone sliced across his ribs.

A blue line of infantry paused on the higher ground in front, to fire on the Rebel infantry at the angle in the fence. But it would not advance.

"Look!" Jamie shouted. "They's perfect targets on the sky!"

The boy fired along with several in the closing companies and the Federal soldiers fell in bunches. But their line held and their return fire was deadly.

One of Pickett's generals crossed the wall where the Union gunners had been driven from their battery and the guns stood silent.

"Come on, Boys, give them the cold steel! Who will follow me?"

He went forward with hat held high on the point of his sword. A rush of men and colors followed him over the wall. Fierce hand-to-hand combat surged about the wall. Infantrymen and artillerymen fought back with rifle butts, hand spikes, and rocks. Men on both sides fired and loaded and fired again. One battery of cannon continued to operate with double loads of canister. But its crew was being thinned at a rapid rate.

As the tide of grey and blue surged and ebbed and mingled in mortal combat, and the air filled with smoke and noise, debris and blood, the few who remained in Company K continued to load and fire on the men in blue. They fought without order. The lieutenant had fallen. Standing, kneeling, pushing through the massed humanity, they did their work.

A flying stone caught Jamie on the head and he went down, blood streaming from a scalp wound. Duane had felt the pull of bullets passing through his clothing, felt the warm dampness of his blood running down his leg and pooling in his shirt, and had heard the missiles of death singing through the air. He knelt to check on Jamie and to load a fresh cylinder into his revolver. The drum sang out as a bullet ripped its head. His companion would be okay. Rising to his feet, he dropped the empty cylinder into his pouch and felt pain seer through his left arm. A bullet had passed through the muscle below his elbow. Blood quickly soaked through his shirt.

There wasn't time for this. The boy moved toward the silent guns for cover. The general who had crossed the wall was gone. Duane saw the general where he lay wounded near the wall. Lead sprayed and burned his cheek as a bullet struck the gun barrel. The blood dripped from the finger tips of his wounded arm as he rested the revolver in his good hand on the gun carriage and fired into the chaotic mass of Federal troops in the trees to the right.

The fragments from the remaining Confederate regiments were falling fast. Some of the colors lay on the ground or were propped against the stonework. Union reinforcements rushed to the scene, but had not yet advanced. Fear held them back. Pain struck Duane's ankle as a sliver of metal cut through his sock. Beyond the trees there was a fierce volley of artillery fire as smoke billowed down the slope and across the stone wall to erase an entire Confederate charge. An eerie silence fell ahead.

Union fire into the mass of grey, mingling leaderless near the angle in the wall, intensified.

"Help me with this gun!" Duane called as he noticed a charge of canister on the ground behind the gun.

Bullets ricocheted from stone and field piece. Suddenly, the powder charge attached to the canister load erupted in flame and smoke. The explosion wrapped around the gun and slammed debris through the drum and the boy's flesh. He felt the heat of the fire and the sting of flying metal. The concussion of explosion wrapped him in pain and the smell of smoke.

Blackness invaded the boy's senses with one grand roaring crescendo and sudden pain.

Then silence. Darkness. Nothing.

*   *   *

Rain fell in sheets. It cascaded from stone walls, gun carriages, and the hat brims of the soldiers wandering the field of carnage. Twenty-four hours before, the sky had unleashed a storm of shot and shell. Now it washed the blood from the grass. Across the landscape the dead and wounded lay where they had fallen or had been able to crawl. Some had tucked themselves into the rocks and crevices of the land, beneath trees and bushes, up against the walls, or underneath the wagons or nearby buildings. The stench of death that had hung about the land was cleansed somewhat by the storm. Still the air was thick with currents of foul odors where the dead lay thickest and the battle had been heaviest. Cries of the wounded had gone silent. Many had passed into eternity. Others had simply become too weak to continue their pleadings. The wreckage of war lay everywhere. Discarded packs and equipment littered the ground. Weapons were scattered about. Exploded artillery chests, unlimbered cannon, wrecked gun carriages, bloated carcasses of horses and mules—all marked the passage of the conflict.

Small groups of men, soaked by the torrential rainfall, searched the muddied landscape for the living. Burial parties gathered the dead in wagons. Some local citizens attempted what they could to help. Scavengers searched the battlefield for souvenirs.

The bodies along the low stone wall near the angle by the clump of trees, were bathed and cleansed by the downpour. Small streams flowed around quiet forms scattered about the landscape. Rivulets trickled along the creases and dips in the fabric which clothed them, to fall with gentle ripplings in the puddles at their side. In the midst of the blue and grey-clad men and boys who carpeted the ground bordered by the angled wall, lay the fallen of Company K. A few had gone back with the retreating survivors. Some had regained strength or consciousness long after the guns fell silent, and waited for darkness in a cloud-banked night sky where the moon lit the hell-scape, then crawled away to hide from the horror.

Lieutenant Damien Jenkins lay among the dead. The bullets had crossed through his lungs, and he had bled to death, his sword still in his hand. Not far away, amidst the layered dead, his cousin Foley had died. A bullet through the heart had made his passing swift. Sergeant Raymond lay outside the wall. His body had been violently torn by the cannon shot. The trail of the dead stretched back to the road and its fences—a carpet of shabby grey and butternut brown in lush green pastures and fertile fields trampled beneath the passing of twelve thousand men.

Beneath the gun, the torrent of rain had puddled about the bodies. The clothing soaked on the still forms, the abundant moisture dripped its washed-out drops of red from edge of collar or coat sleeve, from crumpled hair matted against pale white skin, from fingertips so still. The revolver lay, half submerged, in the red-tinged puddle, not far from the hand that had held it. The boy lay in sodden silence, caressed by trickling falls of water, dripping softly from the gun carriage. One small and intermittent fall played out a steady tapping on the wooden shell of the broken drum which rested in the mud beneath the hub of the wheel.

About this stillness the splash of feet traveled in search of the living and in search of relics. Someone stopped, bent down, and picked the revolver from the water. He moved on, jamming the gun into his waistband and searching for something else of interest. Another paused to take the sword from a dead captain's hand. In awed silence, the footsteps passed on the sodden ground. Some paused to look. Some wept.

The rush of heavy rain wrapped the land in a hushed blanket as the skies wept over the fallen.

Another stopped, as many before him, to look at the sad scene. A boy so young, his shattered drum nearby, lay in the mud not far from the stilled cannon. For some unknowing urgency to caress the child so young, the man knelt down to stroke the soddened locks of brown and matted blood. He was dressed in the long black coat of a reverend. His broad flat-brimmed hat shed the rain in streams. A long charcoal beard dripped water from its carefully groomed point. The long fingers of the shepherd's hands gently pushed the tangled ringlets from the soft cheek.

"Dear, Father," he whispered hoarsely, "why must Your children hurt so? Why must this child die so young?"

The man wept. His tears fell abundantly to mix in the muddied red pool in which he knelt. Again he stroked the cheek, so soft, so cold—his fingers so light against the flesh, so gentle, so caring. The reverend's heart ached with its grief. Oh how he wanted to lift this child's lifeless body from the mud, to hold it, to breathe life back into it. Perhaps if he took it with him he could care for the remains and see that they were buried in the local churchyard. Perhaps he could find out who this boy was and find his family.

Slipping a hand beneath an arm, he froze in astonishment. Why hadn't it occurred to him when he touched the face? It was soft. The arm lay limp. He was alive. The stiffness of death was absent!

"Dearest Father!" the tears flowed in joyous anticipation, "let him live! Let me be your instrument of life!"

Carefully he removed the drumstrap, passed it through a rope stay on the drum, then slung the wooden remains across his back. Gently, the coat-sleeved arms slid beneath the mud, beneath the still body, and lifted the boy from the rain-swept ground beside the silent gun.

Duane hung unconscious in the reverend's arms, his limp form lightened by the long weeks of march. The man carried his burden over the rise in the ground behind the wall to a barn on the back of the ridge where a field hospital was in noisy turmoil. Once inside, the falling rain no longer washed the two, but danced instead in thunderous constancy on the roof overhead.

The interior of the structure was a maze of cots attended by an army of women vivandieres and male nurses, aids, and orderlies. Outside, the bodies of the dead lay in rows, waiting for the burial parties to take them to the cemetery ground for burying. As the reverend entered through the large open door, two men passed on their way out with another who had died on the surgeon's table. Moans and cries of pain blended with dozens of conversations about the cots to mix with the smell of death, excrement, rotting limbs in tubs near the surgeons' tables, smoke, and medicines. For some the barn meant life; for others a pause on the journey to death or the cause of death itself.

A short motherly woman approached the reverend.

"What have you this time, Reverend Smythe?" she asked, wiping her hands on an apron.

"He's just a boy, Mrs. Dowd," he paused for the woman to see. "He's just so pitiful-looking. Truly, I thought he was dead, but the Lord seems to have given a chance for one of His miracles."

"Bring him over here, Reverend." Mrs. Dowd led the way to an empty cot beside the wall. "Just a minute," she said, spreading a blanket across the canvass. "Now put him down." The woman reached across the cot. "Here, let me help."

The two lay Duane on top of the blanket and placed the drum near the head of the spindly frame.

"Let me see if Doc Hurlbut is free to come and look him over." Mrs. Dowd stood and cast a sympathetic smile on the filthy wet figure lying battered and bloody on the bed. "You get his wet things off and gathered in a pile. We'll tend to them later."

The woman hurried off, skirts rustling in her haste, to find a doctor. The man busied himself removing the boy's gear and clothing. Both he and the boy were dripping water from their clothing. The man could not contain the mud and water as he prepared to strip the boy and gather his soaked belongings in a pile. The bed was soaked and dripping through its bottom canvass. The packed dirt floor was puddled about the pile and about the man who worked to help the patient.

Thelma Dowd returned with a basin of water and a bucket of bandages and wash rags.

"He looks so absolutely filthy and smells so. I don't suppose he's had a bath in a month." She emptied the bucket's contents on the floor and settled beside the cot on its overturned bottom.

"It ain't likely, as they've marched all the way from Virginia since the first of last month." He carefully peeled the shirt to reveal the bullet hole in the arm, the shallow gash across the ribs, and sundry other marks and bruises of battle. "Where's Doc?"

"Busy."

Working together, the two did their best to cleanse the weeks of travel and the dirt of battle from the wounded boy. His face was seared and his hair singed from the powder blast. The scalp was bloodied where pieces of the charge had torn through his hat. When finished, Duane was wrapped in a clean dry sheet and moved to a dry cot. Doctor Carl Hurlbut, a local practitioner, joined the effort.

"What do you think is wrong, Doc?" Reverend Smythe inquired. "Why doesn't he respond?"

"He's been burned by a powder blast," the greying physician responded as he carefully examined the wounds about the head through wire-rimmed spectacles. "Could be that he was hit by shell fragments in the head and his hat saved his life. I think his skull is broke or at least banged up pretty bad."

"Serious?" Mrs. Dowd asked.

"Only time will tell." The doctor finished his examination. "Put a salve on the burns, be careful around his eyes, and a poultice on the bullet wounds. Wrap them up and keep them clean. Plenty of rest. Feed him broth or tea until he's fully conscious and can eat." He stood to go. "He's in God's hands, Reverend. All you can do is wait and watch over him."

The doctor packed his bag, smiled a melancholy half smile, then left to continue his work somewhere else in the bustle of the hospital. Duane's treatment was carried out by nurse and reverend. The bandages were wrapped, with extra padding where they crossed his eyes. His belongings were piled beneath the cot. Finally the boy was covered with a light blanket and left to rest. The man and the woman left to care for others while time and God were left to care for the boy.

*　　*　　*

Reverend Leighton Smythe stood just under six feet tall. He was of slender build, stood erect, and generally looked much sterner than he really was. He had been in Gettysburg to visit an aunt when the battle developed. It had not been expected. Neither general had intended to pass through Gettysburg or to occupy the town. It had just happened. Reverend Smythe had gone to the battlefield first out of curiosity, but remained out of a deep feeling of compassion for the men and boys who fell there. Since then, he'd devoted all his waking hours to serving the wounded in the fields and in the hospital.

It had been early afternoon when the reverend walked the battlefield near the angle. Later he had returned to find more who had survived and to help some others to die. Night had fallen. The rain had ended by the time he returned to check on the boy and the other wounded in the hospital barn.

The boy had stirred. Thelma Dowd had checked on him when another reported he was waking. He had moved, but not become conscious. Reverend Smythe stopped to sit a while and to spoon some broth between his lips. Again the boy stirred.

"Thank you, Father," the man prayed quietly. "Stay with him and bring him back."

*   *   *

Duane regained consciousness during the night. He woke to the sounds of moaning in the dark. Discovering himself in bandages, he was confused. But perhaps it was a dream. He went back to sleep to worry about it later.

The early hours of the new day found Mrs. Dowd making her rounds. The boy heard the rustling of her skirts and ventured a question.

"M'am, where am I?" he asked.

The woman stopped, startled by the unexpected voice. It was surprisingly strong. "What?" her voice faltered, tripped by joyful emotion.

"What's happened? Where am I?" He pushed himself up to sit in the middle of the cot. Suddenly aware of his nakedness, he pulled the blanket around himself, then explored with the tips of his fingers to feel the bandages across his eyes.

"Yer in Chamber's barn hospital." The skirts rustled again as she hurried to the side of the bed. There was a milking stool nearby which she brought and placed as a seat. "You were hurt in the great charge. Doc says that your hat saved your life."

133

"What charge?" Duane asked. "Who are ya?"

"Why, I'm Mrs. Dowd. I'm a seamstress here in Gettysburg. What's your name?"

"I'm . . . ," he couldn't remember. "I'm . . . not sure. I cain't git it in ma mind ta say it. But I know's fer sher it's ther. Jest call me Dee. The rest'll come later." He continued to check out the bandages. "Musta bin a mite bad, huh? Sher am wrapped plum up like as some package. Ya use some whiskey 'r brandy? Doc says as it stops the festerin. Gettysburg where?"

"Who says?"

"Cain't rememb'r zactly." A quizzical expression wrinkled around his cheeks. "Ya know, Mrs. Dowd, I cain't seem as ta rememb'r a whole lot."

"You don't remember the war and the fighting? Not even the big battle across the fields the other day?" She put her hand to her chin.

"No, M'am. Seems as ther's somethin' I might a dreamed on, but as all gone fuzzy."

"Well, Dee, I guess we'll just have to get you healed up real fine then see what we can do for your memory later."

"I ain't likin' not knowin', Mrs. Dowd."

"I know, Dee. We'll do as fast as we can."

Reverend Smythe approached on his first visit of the morning. He had just arrived to visit among the patients and was overjoyed to see the boy awake and talking to Mrs. Dowd.

"Good morning, young man," he greeted. "I thank our Father in heaven to see you regaining your strength."

"Mornin', Sir." He turned his head in the direction of the voice.

"We have some work, Reverend," the woman smiled. "This here is Dee, but he's lost his memory for now and can't say that's surely his given name. Dee," she introduced, "this is the Reverend Smythe. He carried you in from the battlefield yesterday."

"Thank ya, Reverend. But I ain't knowin' no battlefield. When kin I gits off these bandagin's an see ya folks? Ya sounds real nice like."

"Thank you, Dee." The nurse went on to explain, "The doc says you were burned in some explosion. We'll wait until he approves, then take them off."

"I have to go back to search for more," the reverend excused himself. "Do you need anything?"

"Yes, Sir," Duane spoke up. "It's real nice yer doin fer me 'n all. But I needs ta git up now 'n agin' an don't feel right, naked as I is. Could ya git me some clothes?"

"I surely can, Son. For now, though, Mrs. Dowd can find you something from about the barn, here."

The man left for his mission on the battlefield. The woman excused herself to her work within the hospital. Nurses were already at work, changing bandages, feeding breakfast of sorts, and visiting with some they had come to know. Nurse Dowd returned later with a clean shirt, then helped Duane to make a needed trip to the privy outside.

It was a slow day for the boy. There was little to do but lie around and wait and listen to the activity of the hospital. When evening arrived, Reverend Smythe returned with a basket for dinner which his aunt had prepared and a clean set of clothes.

First order of business was to get dressed. Then Duane sat on the side of the cot to share dinner of fried chicken, corn, and biscuits. It was heavenly food. He couldn't remember when he'd eaten such food last. Only his mother . . . but she was dead? Why? He pushed the thought from his mind until he could remember what had happened to him and who he was.

"Tell yer aunt as she's a real fine cook. I ain't et so nice since I don't know fer sher."

"You just get your health back. When the bandages come off we'll take you to stay with my aunt until we find your folks and send you home." Reverend Smythe smiled at the boy's good spirits.

"Thank ya, Sir." Duane turned to the woman. "Where's ma thin's? Ya said as I was in a battle?"

"They were a mess," the nurse explained. "I threw them out."

"Could be they'd a he'ped me rememb'r," he suggested.

"True," she agreed. "I'll fetch them home and get them cleaned up for when you're better."

"Thank ya, M'am."

Dinner was finished. The basket was repacked. The boy was free to wander about and to stretch his legs. He was cautious, but glad to be up and out of bed.

*　　*　　*

The days passed. Duane felt his way around and got so he could help with some simple chores to break the monotony. Finally it was time to remove the bandages.

Doctor Hurlbut had changed dressings several times to keep the wounds clean. Now it was his last time to unwrap the boy's head and to let him see again. Mrs. Dowd and Reverend Smythe sat nearby in expectation of seeing their patient without his wrappings. The fabric was removed. The dressing came off the eyes.

"How much longer?" Duane asked, blinking his eyes at the absence of pressure.

"It's done," the doctor said.

"But I cain't see yet?" concern edged his voice.

"I was afraid of that," Doctor Hurlbut stated. "The blast has damaged the eyes. I'm just not sure how bad yet."

"I'm blind?!" the boy cried. "Will I see agin?" His voice became hysterical.

"I really don't know," the doctor said, shaking his head solemnly.

"No!" Duane cried, wringing his hands then rubbing his eyes.

He sat silently, his mouth quivering with fear. The tears came quietly to stream down his cheeks as he shook with inward sobbing.

"I'm sorry," Doc said as he stood to go.

The woman sat down on the bed beside the boy and pulled him into her arms. He broke down and cried violently, burying his tears in her embrace. They both cried.

"Come on," the reverend said softly. "I think it's time you left here, Dee. There's nothing else that my aunt can't do. Let's go home."

"Yes, Sir, Reverend," his voice quavered. "I don't know what fer ta do now. I cain't see. Oh, God, I hope it ain't forev'r." He wiped the tears with his sleeves, then stood beside the cot. "We kin go now?"

"We can go now," Mrs. Dowd assured.

The three stood testily to be sure the boy had his balance. Cautiously they worked their way to the large open door. A friend on either arm guided Duane's footsteps across the hay-strewn floor. Stepping into the mid-morning sunlight, the boy sensed its warmth on his face.

"I kin feel the sun." A smile lit his tear-streaked face.

"That's God's way of saying that there's hope," Reverend Smythe offered.

The trio turned their footsteps towards the town and the home of the reverend's aunt.

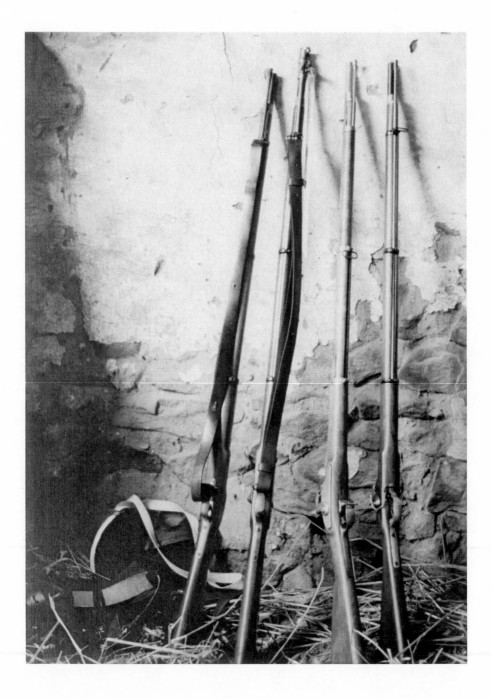

EPILOGUE

Crisp brown leaves danced about the white picket fence that edged the dirt walk in front of the grey, wood-frame house. Broad yellow leaves carpeted the neatly trimmed yard behind the fence where the silver maple tree had shed its summer coat. The raw steel-blue sky of autumn hung over the town with an overcast chill to the air. The summer harvest had been taken in. November was at its mid-point. The war had long since left the country town of Gettysburg and traveled to distant places. Duane Kinkade had not.

Aunt Jennifer Morrison's plain wood-frame house had been home for the boy since the day he left the hospital barn. Here in this tuscan-trimmed, grey clapboard house with its white lace curtains and heavy draped windows, he had learned to cope with blindness and had healed from his wounds. But in the four and a half months he had spent with the Reverend Smythe, he had not found his identity. His past remained a locked secret. Only the brief present held meaning and understanding.

The reverend and his aunt were kind enough. Mrs. Dowd stayed in touch and had taken the boy to spend days with her as she ran errands or worked about her home. The three had helped him learn how to survive the daily routine without the benefit of sight. He became more attuned to his remaining senses as he memorized rooms and frequently traveled locations and developed an ability to feel the presence of people and objects. Aunt Jennifer had put him in a spare bedroom in the front of the house because it faced east and he could feel the sun rise each new day. Duane had become independent in caring for his personal needs and in small household chores such as maintaining his room and helping with meals.

The front door opened. Reverend Smythe and Duane stepped out into the brisk mid-morning air and walked down the flagstone walk toward the rose arbor gate. They proceeded slowly while the boy felt his way with a thin cane stick. Once through the gate, they paused momentarily to listen for passing traffic. One carriage rattled along the empty street.

"Ain't much movin' this time a day," Duane observed.

"I reckon most traffic is staying to the main pikes," the man responded. "But there are greater numbers of curious arriving every day."

Turning right, the duo headed toward the downtown business district beyond the stream which passed under the bridge a block away, and the railroad beyond the bridge.

"What fer we goin' ta Forrester's taday?"

Duane knew the route quite well and moved easily with his hand against the man's elbow.

"I understand he has put up a display of battlefield photographs to draw extra business. People who are coming early for Mr. Lincoln's visit and the cemetery dedication will want to see them."

"Are they all his own pictures?"

"Mostly. Right now he's teaching himself how to use photographic equipment because he plans to sell it. He believes in knowing about the things he sells. He also has a collection of things he's gathered from the battlefield. May be that if you handle some of it, your memory could be helped."

There was a slight arch to the bridge, so Duane knew when they crossed the stream. Just ahead, he heard the bell ringing on the locomotive of a standing train, discharging a new and ever noisy gathering of curious sight-seers.

"Same ol' crowd?" the boy asked.

"Not all of them," Smythe answered. "Looks like quite a few soldiers, too. I figure there'll be a number from the troops being transferred from the west who have heard about this battle and the dedication."

They approached the crowded station overflow. Duane stopped as he sensed several people walking in their direction. The man paused with him.

"It's a big crowd, Dee. I don't blame you for waiting." After standing several minutes in the crowd he added, "Let's sit on this wall for a while, until the mob has passed."

"Good by me," Duane agreed as he turned toward the low stone wall he knew bordered the roadway.

A half hour passed before the two could continue on toward the storefront blocks between the Chambersburg and the York turnpikes. Passersby tipped their hats to the stern-looking reverend with the blind boy, but otherwise ignored them. Dressed in dark woolen trousers with a warm coat and hat over a store-bought shirt, Duane bore no sign of his experience as a soldier. He had become, in fact and even in his own mind, a blind orphan without a background.

The two arrived at Samuel Forrester's Mercantile Store. It's proprietor was one of the many local residents who scavenged the battlefields, even before the armies had gone. He had converted a corner of his storefront into a mini-museum of sorts with weapons and personal items he'd gathered about the countryside, and photographic prints on tin-types which he'd taken throughout the battle.

"Morning, Mr. Forrester," the reverend greeted.

"Hello, Reverend Smythe," the storekeeper approached. "What brings you two in today? You were just here last week."

"We's come ta see yer battle thin's," Duane said cheerfully.

The store was crowded with a noisy invasion of curious visitors. Most had come to see the collection. Most decided to buy something they had not thought to seek, but saw while wandering in the store.

"It's kind of crowded." Mr. Forrester warned. "But you're welcome to stay as long as you like, Dee. May be you'll see or feel something you remember."

"Thanks, Samuel," Leighton smiled. "This was a good idea. Business must be booming."

"That it is—especially in little things like sewing items, soap, buttons, pencils, and the like. I just finished hanging the photographs day before yesterday. Well, got to get back to work."

The storekeeper returned to his counter to be sure the clerks were encouraging sales and to answer visitors' questions about the battle. Duane and the reverend worked the back of the crowd near the special display, allowing themselves to ease toward the front with the flow of moving people. Everyone seemed to be talking at once, commenting on an object or picture, or calling to a wandering child or friend. Duane kept a tight grip on Reverend Smythe's elbow to avoid being separated by the force of the human tide.

"What's it like, Reverend?" the boy asked as he shuffled along beside the man.

"It's a very fine collection, Dee. I surely hope we can get close enough for you to feel some of the pieces of equipment or clothing." The stern countenance of the figure enabled him to ease closer, drawing the boy along, as others gave way in awkward uncertainty. "His tin-types are quite remarkable."

There was an absence of conversation as Reverend Smythe studied the pictures and the boy clung at his side, uncomfortable with the press of people.

The man caught his breath, startled by something. "God have mercy," he whispered. "You're in this picture, Dee."

"Cain't be. I don't even rememb'r eny a this. Though I gotta say as somethin's right there in ma head, jest not clear yet."

"It's you, all right—just like I found you, only early, before it rained."

"Mama!" a small boy at Duane's side called. "Mama, this dead boy's alive. He's right beside me with a preacher-man!"

"Silas," an embarrassed woman reprimanded, "don't be so impolite." She looked at Duane and at the picture. "My heavens, you're right." There was confusion in her tone of voice.

"It's all right, M'am," the man assured. "It is the same boy, but he wasn't killed."

"You're blind!" she exclaimed.

"Yes, M'am," Duane acknowledged.

"Oh, my! Come along, Silas." They moved away.

"I wish I knew what as happened," Duane said. "I wish a knew who I is."

"Let's get a copy of this picture," Reverend Smythe decided. "It may be a help."

They brushed up against an object leaning against the wall which started to move. The boy reached in hope of catching it, but it was moving away from his hand and clattered onto the floor. A short-tempered visitor took notice.

"What's your problem, Boy, clumsy?" a flat-nosed, well-dressed gentleman asked.

"Sher do wish I was, Sir. Truth is I's blind."

"You don't say," the man continued with a sneer.

"You might take a look at this picture," Reverend Smythe pointed. "That's this boy out on the battlefield."

The man stared hard as surprise and embarrassment registered in flush pink on his cheeks. "Oh," he said quietly, then turned and walked away.

"Everything okay?" Mr. Forrester asked, hurrying across at the appearance of commotion.

"Yes, Sir," the boy said, "if I didn't break nothin'."

"It was a pole of some sort," he retrieved the object. "Here, nothing broken." The storekeeper took the boy's hand and put the object into it.

The reverend watched hopefully as the boy ran his fingers along the slender shape. "It's a trail handspike fer movin' a cannon ta aim it."

"Well I'll be," his guardian smiled. "I do believe your mind is going to let you know yourself." The boy's smile of pride was mixed with tears of grateful hope. "Mr. Forrester," the man continued, "I'd like a copy of this photograph. It's Dee, here, from the battlefield."

The storekeeper-photographer took a serious look at his photograph. "Why it surely is." There was surprise in his voice. "I'll make a copy this evening and you can pick it up tomorrow."

"Thank you," the reverend stated. "I think we'll stay a while longer to see what else is familiar. Then we'll go our way and I'll be back tomorrow."

The two stayed and explored the exhibit while the storekeeper returned to his business. There was a new excitement as the boy recognized much of what he touched and felt a sense of joyful expectation that soon he might remember who he really was.

*   *   *

The small, white-haired Aunt Jennifer washed the dishes in the porcelain basin and set them carefully on the towel-covered drain board. One by one, Duane searched out each piece, dried it, and placed it toward the back of the surface in a safe pile. Leighton Smythe was seated at the table preparing a letter to a church in Richmond requesting help in identifying the boy in the picture to be enclosed.

Outside, the broken moon was rising in the east as the last twilight of the day was fading in the west. A chill air was gathering in the evening. Somewhere a cat yowled. Otherwise the neighborhood on the northeast corner of town was quiet.

There was a warmth of companionship in the kitchen as each worked in the other's presence and Duane and Aunt Jennifer's nephew shared the story of the day's discoveries. The fire crackled cheerily in the kitchen range, its snapping to blend with the dripping wash water cascading from the woman's hands to play a symphony of sound in the boy's mind which, deprived of sight, cherished the rich blend of noise. An unexpected rapping on the front door interrupted the routine of harmony. The boy heard it first and stopped in the middle of his statement.

"Afta we was done with the rifle, the reverend put . . . thar's a knockin' on the door, Sir."

Everyone paused mid-motion. The ticking of the parlor clock was being joined by a series of rappings on the door.

"I'll see who it is," the man said as he stood from the table. "You two go on."

But curiosity had the better of boy and woman who paused in their work as they tried to listen. They could hear a murmur of conversation as the man opened the door and stepped out to talk to the visitor.

"God be praised!" they heard him exclaim.

"Who do you suppose it could be, Dee," Aunt Jennifer asked.

"Cain't hear em much. Don't rightly know," he answered.

Footsteps approached the kitchen.

"Wait here a minute," the reverend stated before entering the room. "Duane Kinkade, I know who you are!" The thrill of ecstatic triumph filled his voice. He was almost crying.

"What!" the woman gasped.

"Thet sher sounds right, but where'd ya hear?"

"I told him, Dee," the officer stepped into the room.

"The voice!" Duane nearly cheered. "I know ya!" he exclaimed. "Lieutenant! Lieutenant Dan Marshalton! Oh, God! Oh, God! Ya cain't know how happy I is!" The boy broke into tears as he stumbled against the chair in his eagerness to reach the man.

Another entered the room quietly and stood in respectful silence as the boy and the officer embraced. Both had given way to tears and hugs. Then Duane froze.

"It's Johnny!" He could say no more, only reach toward the presence he felt so close.

Johnny stood transfixed at the sight of his blinded friend, but moved at a nod from Reverend Smythe. He held his hand to touch Duane's outstretched fingers. They met and the younger boy pulled at his friend. The three embraced each other as the reverend went to stand with his aunt. She was bawling into her apron. Her nephew stood with the tears cascading silently down his cheeks. The boy and his friends held onto each other as if afraid to let go and sobbed uncontrollably for several minutes.

When all had finally regained their composure, the lieutenant was the first to speak.

"I believe this is yours, Reverend Smythe." He offered a large flat paper envelop. "Mr. Forrester said I could bring it over since I was coming."

"Thank you, Captain Marshalton."

"Captain?" the boy asked.

"Yes, Dee, I finally got a promotion."

"But, Captain," Leighton continued, "I won't be needing this now and can get another if I wish. You keep it for Dee."

"Would you all like to set in the parlor?" Aunt Jennifer offered. "I'll put on a pot of coffee and you can share the making of this miracle."

She wiped her eyes on her apron, then reached down a coffee tin in which she kept her ground coffee. As the reverend shepherded the boy and his friends toward the parlor, his aunt pumped a pot of water from the kitchen sink and prepared the pot to be placed on the hot kitchen range. Then she, too, moved to join the others and satisfy her curiosity as to the identity of the boy she had kept these past four months.

Captain Marshalton had taken the velvet green gentleman's chair, offered by his host. Johnny and Duane had settled on the elegantly upholstered settee. Reverend Smythe was comfortable in a platform rocker. Aunt Jennifer joined them in her high-backed Boston rocker.

The captain had already begun, ". . . and decided to see what he had. It was Johnny who saw the picture. He asked me to look at it and say what I thought. I knew from the expression on his face that he was very upset. As soon as I saw him I knew inside it was Dee, even though this doubt kept poking at my mind. You can't imagine the awful agony we felt, believing he was dead, or the sudden joy when we asked Mr. Forrester about the picture and he told us he was alive. He was shocked as were we at the coincidence of our meeting and was obviously proud to be able to tell us all he knew. Then he gave me the copy you had ordered and told us how to get here."

"I cain't b'lieve it," Duane said. "I ain't been knowin' who I was all this time, but jest as soon as I heard yer voice, ever'thin' come back. Ever'thin' that is but ma eyes."

"Do you have any idea about them?" Johnny asked.

The boy replied, "The doctor says as he thinks I'll neve' see agin. But then I guess I's still lucky. I should a been kilt by them pieces a canister shot."

"God works his miracles," Leighton praised.

"That he does," the captain agreed. There was a moment of quiet before he continued. "I know you two want to learn more about Dee and I'm going to let him tell it. But now we must decide his future."

"I want ta go with ya, whereve' yer headin'," Duane stated. "I know it ain't no place fer a blind boy, but if there's some way ya kin git me ta the Confederate Army an find ma pa, I wanna go, no matter how long it takes."

"There's a relatively recent serious move in establishing what's called the Invalid Corps." Captain Marshalton leaned forward in the chair with his elbows on his knees. "It allows for wounded or ineligible soldiers to work in non combat areas like supply or hospitals or prison camps. I don't know as there're any blind soldiers in such a position, but I will certainly try to do what I can."

"Would it help if you were the boy's legal guardian?" the reverend asked.

"It has had its advantages with Johnny."

"I have some friends over at the courthouse. I'll see to the paperwork."

"Captain," Mrs. Morrison joined in, "would you and Johnny care to stay here while you're in Gettysburg? I've yet another room and you're welcome to it."

"That would be wonderful, Mrs. Morrison. We certainly would."

147

"I smell coffee," Johnny interrupted.

"Coming right up." The woman rose from her rocker and went to get the coffee.

"We'll help," Duane offered.

"Sure," Johnny added.

The two hurried to join her.

"He does get along well," Dan observed, watching Duane maneuver about the house.

As the evening passed, arrangements were made for Duane's immediate future and for the captain and Johnny to settle in for the next several days. They had come to witness the dedication of the new cemetery as they were transferring commands from the army in Tennessee to the Army of the Potomac. The war in the west was nearly won.

The new effort was to stop General Lee's Army of Northern Virginia. Once business was concluded, the gathering settled to coffee with cookies and Duane's tale to the reverend and his aunt as to who he was and where he had been in the war. Dan and Johnny were also very interested in all he had done since the last battle in Tennessee. Widow Smith had informed them that he had headed off to Bragg's army and they had assumed that he had made it. Yet, they had hoped to hear for sure and became concerned as time passed that something had gone wrong.

The visit lasted late into the night. Mrs. Morrison added some wood to the parlor stove to keep off the autumn chill as the boys helped return the dirty dishes to the drainboard. The parlor clock struck the hour at eleven. Dan and Johnny would bring their things from their boarding house in the morning. They would spend this night in their new guest accommodations.

The stoves were banked. Candles were lit for the trip up to bed. The lamps were put out. All retired to their rooms, still chattering in exhausted excitement and the wonder of the reunion. The boy said good night to Dan and Johnny. They were shown to their room and he went on to his.

As Duane changed into his night shirt, he listened to the sounds of the rest of the household settling in for the night. How good it was to be with his friends once again. But more than that, how thankful he felt to have come out of the darkness of his lost memory and to rediscover who he was. Feeling his way to the bed, the boy pulled the covers down and crawled in. The house quieted. But Duane lay awake, listening to the house's noises as he thought of what had been and what might yet be. His mind relaxed. He drifted into a restful sleep and dreams of hope.

About the author, J. Arthur Moore

J. Arthur Moore is an educator with 42 years experience in public, private, and independent settings. He is also an amateur photographer and has illustrated his works with his own photographs. In addition to *Journey into Darkness*, Mr. Moore has written *Summer of Two Worlds*, "Heir to Balmawr", a drama for his fifth grade students, a number of short pieces, and short stories. His latest work is a short story titled "West to Freedom."

A graduate of Jenkintown High School, just outside of Philadelphia, Pennsylvania, he attended West Chester State College, currently West Chester University. Upon graduation, he joined the Navy and was stationed in Norfolk, Virginia, where he met his wife to be, a widow with four children. Once discharged from the service, he moved to Coatesville, Pennsylvania, began his teaching career, married and brought his new family to live in a 300-year-old farm house in which the children grew up and married, went their own ways, raised their families to become grandparents themselves.

Retiring after a 42-year career, Mr. Moore has moved to the farming country in Lancaster County, Pennsylvania, where he plans to enjoy the generations of family and time with his model railroad, and time to guide his writings into a new life through publication. It also allows time for traveling to Civil War events, presenting at various organizations and events, time with adopted grandchildren (five former students who were key to the 6-month move project and have become family), and, having saved the camp equipment from years of programs with schools and in the summer, the chance to build a camp site in the back yard for the kids.

Edwards Brothers Malloy
Thorofare, NJ USA
April 15, 2013